TRUST IN ME

SIERRA CARTWRIGHT

HAWKEYE

TRUST IN ME

DEDICATION

For YOU! I appreciate you taking the time to read the Hawkeye series, books of my heart.

Tanja, Aimz, and Katherine, I appreciate your fabulous feedback. Thank you!

BAB, I love ya and appreciate you.

.

CHAPTER ONE

HAWKEYE

Aimee adjusted her earbuds, then headed toward the front door for her late-afternoon run. It'd been a hell of a day, and she needed the stress relief. She turned the knob, then screamed. A large, gorgeous man stood on her porch, arms folded across his broad chest.

Stunned, and more scared than she would ever admit, she froze.

He moved toward her, galvanizing her into action. She took an immediate step back, then shoved against the door to slam it.

"Wait!" He placed his booted foot in the entrance, blocking her efforts. Not just a booted foot, she noted wildly —a massive one, with the black leather riding boots showing nicks and scars—from a life on the edge if her guess was correct.

Her pulse slammed into overdrive.

Crap, crap, crap.

"I'm Trace Romero," the man said, pushing back against her.

Would a potential bad guy introduce himself? Her older

sister carried a gun while Aimee was the nerd with the iPod, ponytail, and a scientific mind that rarely shut down. They were both employed by Hawkeye Security, but since Aimee worked in IT, she'd never gone through firearms or specialized tactical training programs.

"I'm from Hawkeye. Your sister sent me to stay with you for a few days."

Her breath whooshed out.

She should be relieved, but she wasn't.

Two hours prior, she'd returned from the coffee shop to find the back patio door slightly ajar. Concerned, she'd notified her sister. The fact that an agent was standing on Aimee's porch meant her sister had called out the cavalry in the form of one of their colleagues.

And she didn't want him here. Hawkeye was one of the planet's most exclusive security firms. They hired only the most qualified operatives, recruiting from the military and police, even the FBI or Secret Service.

But that didn't matter to her. She had no intention of letting an arrogant alpha male inside her home. She'd learned her lesson with know-it-all men, and she was too smart to repeat the mistake.

"Please step back, ma'am. Ms. Inamorata is expecting a report from me."

"You can tell her you were here and that I sent you away. Mission accomplished."

"I'm afraid I can't do that. If I don't answer your phone when she calls, I might as well turn in my resignation and throw myself off Pikes Peak, save her the effort of hunting down my sorry carcass."

Aimee's running shoes slipped as he threw his strong shoulder into the door. For all the success her efforts were having at keeping him out, she might as well be trying to hold back an avalanche.

Maybe she couldn't beat him when it came to physical strength, but she could batter his ego and get under his defenses. "I can't believe a big, strong man is frightened of my sister."

"Terrified, actually. Like all mortals," he confessed.

"Damn." She groaned. His ego was intact enough for him not to rise to her bait.

"You have two choices, ma'am." His deep voice was controlled and clipped. "We can do it my way." He paused for a couple of beats, then added, "Or we can do it my way."

She hated having people in her space. It was bad enough sharing the fifteen hundred square feet with her rescue parrot that rarely shut up, but having someone around who would watch her television, eat her food, discover her deepest secrets…

The brute of a man nudged her back another few inches. "It's okay to stop the badass act." But a panicky little part of her was afraid it wasn't an act at all.

"Step away from the door, Miss Inamorata." This warning wasn't as friendly as the previous one had been.

So maybe she didn't carry a gun, but she'd learned a few things from listening to her sister. If you can't go through, go around. "Okay. You win."

He stopped pushing. She counted to two. When he let down his guard, she grunted and then shoved forward with every scrap of determination she could summon.

But her pissed-off best wasn't good enough.

His foot was still firmly lodged in the entrance.

Within seconds, he filled the space.

Good God, he was big. Bigger than big.

Instinctively she took a protective step back. No matter how mad she was, she would never be able to win against this man.

He dominated the space and sucked up the air she'd been

intending to breathe. He stood well over six feet tall, and his shoulders almost filled the width of the opening.

She, who rarely got flustered, was immobilized. Agent Romero made her oh so aware of being a woman. In her shorts and tiny tank top, she felt small, vulnerable, while he was spectacular, from his angular cheekbones to his military-precise haircut and rich, deep brown eyes. His skin revealed a Spanish heritage, and it might have been a shade or two richer for having been in the sun. His strong jaw was set in an implacable line. In every way, he spelled danger.

He took her shoulders, moved her back a foot, then released her long enough to turn, slam the door, and turn the lock…all before she could even draw a protesting breath.

"My way," he reminded her.

From the other room, Eureka squawked.

"What the hell is that?"

She should probably warn him about Eureka, her blue-fronted Amazon parrot, but it would be much more fun if he found out himself. "It's my bird."

"Inside? A pet?"

"He thinks he's the boss around here."

"Anything else I need to know?"

"I'm pretty boring." She shrugged.

"Not if someone broke in."

"Maybe I left the patio door ajar myself." But that couldn't possibly be true. Because she wanted to keep Eureka safe, she was careful to keep all possible escape places closed.

"The local police said there have been no other reported break-ins, and I understand nothing was taken?"

"That's true." Her electronics were still in place. None of her jewelry was missing. Even her emergency stash of twenty-dollar bills remained untouched in her dresser drawer.

"Which means it wasn't a random thing, and you and Ms. Inamorata know it. Want to show me around?"

"No. Not really," she said, not even trying to disarm her words with a smile.

"You can show me, or I can look myself."

His way. Or his way. "There's not much to see. My bedroom, which you're not going into, my office, which you're not going into, the kitchen, dining room, the guest bathroom, and my living room...which you're standing in. That's it."

He took another step toward her.

The scent of him seared her, like a cool Colorado breeze wrapped in the spice of night.

Reluctantly she ceded the ground. Just as fast, she regretted her action. Instead of remaining where he was, Trace took another step in her direction. This time she forced herself to stand still. She crossed her arms across her midriff, fighting the natural instinct to get the hell away from him.

"I'll show myself around."

"Fine." She angled her chin in false bravado. "I'll just go for my run while you have a look-see. Be gone when I return." As she started past him, he snagged her wrist firmly enough to say he meant business.

"I've been assigned to protect you. You run, I run."

Her patience snapped. "Me Tarzan, you Jane."

"Yeah. Something like that."

She snatched her wrist away from him, pretending her heart wasn't thundering. She wouldn't need a cardio workout if he stayed under her roof another five minutes. His touch bothered her. His aggressive style bothered her. But what concerned her most was her own way too feminine reaction to him. "You're interrupting my schedule, Mr. Romero—Agent Romero. Whatever your name is."

"Trace."

She exhaled. He'd said it softly, a whisper of seduction. "You won't be here long enough for us to get that familiar."

"Don't count on it."

"Look, I appreciate what you're trying to do—"

"What I've been *ordered* to do."

"My sister overreacted, probably because *I* overreacted."

"Ms. Inamorata doesn't overreact." Patience wove through his tone. Maybe because he knew he would win. "If she thinks someone should protect your body and your secrets"—his glance started at her head and slowly traveled downward, igniting too-long-dormant senses—"then I'm going to be here for as long as she says."

"The police said they'd be happy to drive by."

"Periodically." He nodded. "But they're not going to provide the kind of protection I can."

"But—"

"Listen, Miss Inamorata. I'm here. And I don't need your permission to stay."

She tightened her ponytail. "Can I finish a sentence?"

"Depends whether you're going to agree with me or not." He grinned then, and strange things happened to her insides. "For the record," he continued, "there are other ways to shut you up. Who knows?" He leaned in a bit closer. "You might enjoy them. I would."

What the hell? No. Her heart increased its tempo to at least eighty-five percent of her target heart rate. She told herself he wouldn't kiss her, told herself she wouldn't let him if he tried.

The phone rang, mercifully shattering the moment.

"That'll be your sister, for me."

The phone trilled a second time.

She sighed. "Through there," she said, pointing toward the

6

kitchen. It wasn't lost on her that he had won every battle thus far.

He nodded and headed into the heart of her home.

She trailed him, fully intending to eavesdrop.

"Bombs away!"

Scowling, Trace turned to look at her.

"Eureka!" she commanded. "No. *God, no.*

The incessant phone, the shrieking bird, her tension, all created sudden pandemonium. From everywhere at once, Eureka flew into the room, a fury of feathers and obnoxious squawks.

"Duck!" she warned.

Too late.

Eureka swooped low over Trace's head.

Aimee pushed her palms against her eyes, unable to watch.

"Crap!"

Her word exactly.

"Return to base," the parrot cried. "Return to base!"

The phone stopped ringing. Eureka landed on the perch on top of his cage. He rang a bell that hung beneath a mirror. "Mission accomplished!" Then silence, sudden and oppressive, echoed.

"Sorry about that," she said, slowly pulling her hands away from her face. "I should have warned you about his...tendencies."

"Does he do that a lot?"

"Only when he's upset. Hopefully he got the intruders. Bastards for leaving a door open, anyway. If anything happened to him—"

"I think he's okay," Trace said drily.

She was glad for his interruption. That ridiculous, bad-mannered bird was her best friend.

"Did he get me?" Trace ran a hand across the top of his head, then looked at his palm.

"You'll need to change your shirt," she said. For the first time, she smiled at him. "Since you probably don't have another one, you can just go home."

"Stubborn woman."

"Stubborn man," she countered.

"It will wash." He dragged the hem from the waistband.

"Err…"

He exposed part of his stomach, showing off his tight abs. *Damn.* Then he pulled the shirt a bit higher. "Don't!" she begged. "Please." Having him this close was bad enough. Half-naked would undo her.

The phone rang again. Looking at Trace, Eureka lifted a foot from the perch, as if considering his options.

"Eureka, no," she warned. He put his foot back down. "Good boy." But she, too, had her eye on Trace as he continued to the kitchen. His boots were loud on her hardwood floor, and as large as he was, he dwarfed the space.

On the third ring, Trace picked up her phone. "Romero." He looked at her as he spoke to her sister. "No, ma'am. She hasn't been the least bit hospitable. I have a bruised foot and parrot shit on my shirt."

Rat bastard.

"Yeah, no problem." He held out the phone toward her.

Reluctantly she crossed to him, not wanting to get any closer to him than she needed to. Her mind might not have wanted him in her space, but her body most definitely did.

She took the device from him and, to her sister, said, "Hey."

He stood there, watching as her sister gave Aimee hell, finishing with, "We don't know what's going on. You have to think about yourself *and* the project."

"Exactly," Aimee agreed. Each day, the team drew closer

to making the whole project work together. And the world would change when they succeeded. "Now you see the issue. I can't work with someone breathing down my neck."

"Is that what he's doing?"

Actually he *was* close enough that she could feel the warmth of him. And it wasn't all terrible. But it sure as hell was a distraction.

"I'm sure he'll do his best to stay out of your way."

"In a house this small? That's not possible."

"It's either Trace, or I will move you to a safe house. That's actually my preference."

"That would be traumatic for Eureka," Aimee protested.

"Those are your only choices, Aimee."

Aimee was the scientist, calm and rational, or she had been until ten minutes ago when Tall, Dark, and Dangerous showed up on her porch. She sighed.

"Do it for me?"

Trace's penetrating gaze was still on Aimee, heating her blood. "This is under duress."

"So noted."

She hung up.

"The formidable Ms. Inamorata wins another round?" His arms were folded across his chest, and he didn't gloat.

"Could you look smug or triumphant or something? It would be easier to dislike you that way."

"Surprisingly, some people like me."

She couldn't afford to be one of them, as easy as that promised to be with him standing only inches away and smelling so damn good. "You're right. That is surprising."

"When I first got here, I checked out the front of the house and the backyard. I wish you had a privacy fence rather than a chain-link one."

"The neighbors have a dog."

"Good to know. Now let's get the grand tour over with."

Did he ever give up? "You still need to wash your shirt."

"I have a duffel bag in my vehicle."

"Why am I not shocked?"

"Deductive reasoning? I understand you're a scientist."

"There is that." She couldn't help but smile. He was as charming as he was uncompromising.

"I fully intended to stay, regardless of your reception. I have workout clothes as well."

"But if we both go for a run, no one will be protecting the house."

"Wrong again. Your sister has assigned a couple of details. Bree Mallory and Daniel Riley are stationed in an SUV down the block. There's another team at the entrance to the subdivision."

"She thinks of everything."

He headed for the front door. "Be back in less than thirty seconds."

Aimee thought about locking him out, but the dark glance he shot her, combined with that set of his jaw, promised retribution if she crossed him. *His way.*

Standing in the doorway, she watched him jog across the road to his ridiculously large badass SUV. It resembled a military vehicle, capable of climbing anything or plowing through a lake. Faded denim hugged his powerful thighs and showed off his long legs. But if she were honest, she'd admit she liked the way they fit his taut ass. It appeared to be as nicely shaped and as honed as the rest of him.

Aimee mentally gave herself a shake. She shouldn't be having fantasies about her temporary jailer.

After grabbing an army-green duffel bag from the passenger seat, Trace slammed the door. He gave a thumbs-up signal to a white Suburban parked down the street— Mallory and Riley, he assumed—before jogging back to her.

Aimee took a step back to let him into the house.

"Should I change in your bedroom?"

"That's off-limits, I told you."

Right there, in the entryway, he pulled off the black cotton shirt.

She should have known better than to forbid him to do something.

Carefully he wadded the T-shirt. Even though she tried not to look, she was mesmerized. As she'd already surmised, he was seriously one sexy man. He had no excess fat around the middle, and a smattering of dark hair arrowed down the center of his chest to disappear behind the brass button holding his jeans together.

Her pulse easily reached eighty-seven, maybe eighty-eight, percent of her target heart rate. She didn't need her fitness monitor to tell her that. "I'll, uhm, throw that in the washer."

He handed her the T-shirt, then bent to unzip his bag.

"Is that a freaking gun tucked in your waistband?"

"Yeah," he said.

"No. No guns in my house. No way, no how."

He sighed, but he didn't stop riffling through his bag. And heaven help her, she couldn't help but cast a surreptitious glance at the contents, looking to see if he had underwear there. He pulled out a replacement black shirt, but she didn't see any boxers, briefs, or tighty whities. That realization revved her libido into overdrive.

"I mean it, Trace. No weapons."

He stood. "I appreciate that you don't want me here. I realize having a gun in your house is uncomfortable. I know I'll be invading your privacy."

"And?"

"Tough."

"Tough?"

He took her by the shoulders. "Tough."

11

When he released her, she slumped.

How did everything get to be so out of control? She hated this, despised all of Hawkeye Security at the moment.

Needing to do something useful, something she could control, she pulled away from him to head down the hallway to the bathroom that also served as a laundry room.

A man in her house. Protective detail. A damn pistol. This morning, life had been blessedly normal, but now nothing was.

She turned on the washer to the smallest load setting. In the nearby basket, there were some dark clothes that she could wash, but throwing their stuff in together seemed too intimate.

When she was in college, she'd fallen madly in love with Jack Cotter, a man significantly older than her. He was a trial lawyer, confident and sophisticated, so different from the techie geeks she hung out with.

He'd proposed, and she'd accepted and been swept into a world she didn't understand. He bought her a new wardrobe and expected her to help him entertain his clients, sacrificing her school work for his ambitions. Within six months, she lost herself, cutting back the number of classes she enrolled in, no longer seeing her friends, always being available for Jack and his demands.

When her sister returned from a long assignment, she'd been concerned about Aimee's well-being, but Aimee hadn't been ready to end the relationship.

After Jack took her phone and changed the number to keep the sisters apart, Aimee was finally able to see what was happening. Her sister was the only relative she had, and she couldn't imagine a life without her.

Weeks before the wedding, while Jack was embroiled in the trial of the century, Aimee fled. Even though she'd gotten away, it had taken her months to rediscover who she was, and make up the work she'd missed to graduate on time.

She'd vowed never again to allow a man to take over her life.

Deciding to wash her own clothes later, Aimee dropped the lid on the machine, then returned to her office and closed the door. She was aware of Trace's movements as he went through her house, coldly invading her privacy.

Even though she'd banned him from her office, he entered after a perfunctory knock. Jaw locked to hold back her temper, she looked up at him. "Can I help you with something?"

"Just need to have a quick look around."

"For what?"

"Anything out of the ordinary. A bug, potentially. Something planted on your computer."

She hadn't considered that possibility. More than anyone on the planet, she should have. A hardware hack was difficult, but not impossible.

"You don't have to stay," he said.

As if she'd leave. Aimee remained where she was, watching his every move.

He was thorough. He flipped through her stacks of notes, shook her pens, looked under the desk, opened drawers and the closet doors, looked behind the curtains, checked the window. He pulled the cord on the drapes and said, "Leave them closed, if you don't mind."

Since she liked natural sunlight, she did mind, not that it mattered.

When he slid aside her Georgia O'Keeffe print, her hold on her anger began to fray. "Have you seen enough?"

"Doing my job. We need to check your computer."

"I'll do it myself."

After a nod, he left, and she remained where she was,

breathing in his scent, willing away his lingering presence. A minute later, realizing she hadn't moved, she stood and crossed the room to nudge the O'Keeffe print back into place. Then she checked her computer and ran a diagnostic.

If she couldn't run, she could work, or at least pretend to do something useful.

CHAPTER TWO

HAWKEYE

adre de Dios.

M Trace hadn't been sure what to expect when Ms. Inamorata summoned him to her office a couple of hours ago. She was always composed, calm under pressure, which was why Hawkeye trusted her implicitly and had made her part of his inner circle. Whenever a situation got out of hand, she could be counted on to deal with local and federal authorities, smoothing over all the details. According to Hawkeye, she batted cleanup better than any major leaguer.

So when Trace saw her, blonde hair mussed as if she'd dragged a hand through it, worrying a pen between her teeth, he'd taken a seat and never considered refusing the request to look after her younger sister, a part-time adjunct professor who was working on a top secret project for an unnamed Hawkeye client. Inamorata had declined to provide any further information, but added that she would clear Aimee to share details if she wanted to.

Inamorata confessed she was perplexed by the break-in. Nothing had been taken, or so it appeared. Theoretically, no one knew who Aimee was. As far as friends and neighbors were concerned, she taught at the college and worked on educational software.

Bad guys shouldn't know of her existence.

But still, Ms. Inamorata wasn't willing to take any unnecessary risks.

Despite Aimee's protests that she didn't need protection, it wouldn't hurt to monitor the situation. Her routine was predictable. She rarely went out, except for her latte and daily exercise. This semester, she wasn't teaching.

He'd expected Aimee's fiery protests when he arrived, but nothing could have prepared him for the sight of her sculptured body or his intense physical reaction to her. It was a force of its own, startling and demanding, as unwelcome as it was unexpected.

Shaking his head to clear it, he opened her bedroom door. Like the rest of the house, it was uncluttered. Her bed was made, and soft, feminine pillows adorned the bright pink quilt. With determination, he shoved aside the thought of taking her on it, exorcising the need that consumed him.

Trace strode to her closet. It, too, was exactly what he expected. She had half a dozen pairs of running shoes, some dress sandals, lots of outdoor and sports gear, and a tennis racquet. She didn't have many clothes hanging there, just a few pairs of slacks, several skirts, a number of blouses, and a bunch of sleeveless shirts. The slinky black dress tucked in the corner intrigued him, and he had to forcibly remind himself he was here for work. If he'd met her at the annual holiday party, things would have been different…much different.

He crouched in front of her bookcase. Half a shelf of self-help titles. A couple of text books, a few bestsellers, and on the bottom right, an extensive collection of erotic fiction along with two respected how-to manuals about BDSM.

Fuck.

Aimee Inamorata had carnal interests that matched his own.

Double fuck. This was dangerous knowledge. He had no business thinking about her in a sexual way.

He moved to her dresser, checked beneath her jewelry box, behind picture frames. Then he went through her drawers. No surprises. Sturdy undergarments, workout gear, shorts and T-shirts, a few pairs of jeans, a couple of sweatshirts.

The bottom drawer, however, contained frivolous panties and lingerie.

An image of her dressed in the black scraps of material floated through his mind. He reminded himself she was a job, an assignment.

After running his fingers along the sides and bottom panel, he checked out her nightstand, picking up a lamp to feel along the base. Satisfied, he tugged open the single drawer and discovered her personal toys—a vibrator, a pair of nipple clamps, and a small metal butt plug.

Goddamn it.

He shoved that drawer closed with far too much force, then got the hell out of the room.

For a moment, he paused in the hallway.

Then, demanding professionalism of himself, Trace went through every item in her living room and kitchen. An hour later, he headed for the back patio door, intending to take another trip around the exterior of the house. The crazy *loro* jumped down from the top of his cage and began a ridiculous waddle walk toward the opening. "Stay." Did birds respond the same way dogs did?

He closed the door and swept the backyard from left to right, looking for anything that was different from an hour ago. He hopped the chain-link fence, went to exchange a few words with the Hawkeye agents in the SUV, and then circled behind her evergreen trees.

Everything checked clear.

Since the front door was closed, he returned to the back-yard, this time using the gate. It squeaked, which he appreci-ated. One more sound to be aware of.

He entered the house, and Aimee stood in the kitchen, a glass of water in her hand.

"You were right that you were going to invade my privacy."

She had no idea how much. In his pocket, his phone vibrated, and he checked the message screen. "Hawkeye is sending over a few techs to look for prints, examine the scene."

"The scene? You mean my *home?*"

"Look, Aimee." Impatience snapped through him. But when he looked into the cornflower blue of her eyes, an unfamiliar seed of compassion seeped in. She might be a fellow operative, but new recruits in accounting and IT were not required to go through physical or firearms training. She was working on a top secret project, but the break-in and the invasion of her privacy had to be stressful.

Something in him softened, and he allowed his heart to lead. "Earlier, you were headed out for a run. Give me five minutes to change, and we can go." Being out of the house while strangers picked through it—like he had done—might be easier for her.

"I thought you were going to keep me imprisoned."

"Think of me as a companion."

"A companion?" She scoffed. "That's adorable."

"Your call." Her reaction annoyed him, but he tamped it down. "We can go for a run." He shrugged. "Or we can discuss your reading material while we wait for the team to arrive."

"My…" She turned half a dozen shades of scarlet, and she wrapped her arms around her middle as if to protect herself.

He cursed himself. He had no right to comment on her personal belongings or life. It was more than unprofessional, it was foolish.

"My BDSM books? Perhaps you noticed the murder mysteries as well." Her voice was cool, more controlled than he'd imagined it would be. "According to your logic, that must mean I know at least a dozen ways to kill a man and dispose of his body." Her grin was wicked.

"Touché."

Silence drew as they squared off. "I don't want anyone in the house unless I'm here. Eureka's had enough stress."

"And so have you. Let the team in while we're gone. Can he go in his cage or something?" When she didn't respond, he pressed again. "It has to happen. The sooner we get it over with, the faster your life returns to normal."

"I hate this."

"I don't blame you." His tone held sympathy, something unusual for him.

Maybe she sensed that because she sighed and then relented. "Five minutes."

He grabbed his duffel and dug out his workout clothes. He considered where to change, opting for the bathroom.

Within three minutes, he was ready to go. Less than thirty seconds later, she was closing Eureka into his cage, promising to return soon. Maybe as a peace offering, she gave the bird a piece of an orange.

"He can't escape, can he?" He eyed the menace.

"So far, he hasn't managed to figure that out." She programmed her fitness watch. "Are you going to be able to keep up?"

He regarded her. It didn't sound like a challenge, just a question of interest. "How far do you plan to go?"

"Seven-minute miles." She inserted a pair of wireless earbuds, turned on some music, then grinned at him. "Less than an hour. You do the math."

It was a fair pace. "I'll do my best."

He did well, until she started up the trail on Green Mountain. His last assignment had been at sea level. The altitude, combined with the elevation gain, kicked his ass. The perky Miss Inamorata continued to lead the way, ponytail bobbing, music thumping out a distant up-tempo beat, not breathing hard.

Twice, she'd taught him not to underestimate her.

Downhill was better, at least on his cardiovascular system. But it was hell on his knees.

She arrived at the trailhead ahead of him, and she was jogging in place, wearing a triumphant grin when he stopped beside her, struggling to breathe.

"That wasn't so bad, was it?"

"Walk in the park." His ego made him lie.

On the way back, she slowed the pace a little. He didn't let her see his gratitude.

A few blocks from the house, she shut off her music, tapped the screen of her watch, studied the information, then glanced about him. "So tell me about you, Trace."

"Pretty boring life."

"Well, you're damn nosy. I know that much. You dug through all of my belongings, looked at my whole life."

Not all of it. But enough to intrigue the hell out of him.

"Fair's fair. I should know something about the man who's going to be sleeping under my roof."

"Not much to know. Been with Hawkeye about five years. Properly vetted by your sister."

"Any wife waiting for you to come home?"

"No."

"Girlfriend?"

The memory had lost its burn over the years, but the lesson remained. His need for adrenaline and a meaningful relationship couldn't exist in the same space. "It was a long time ago."

"Was it the job? That happens."

"In a way. More than anything, I suppose, the problem was me." The admission hurt. And it was the first time he'd made it aloud.

"Ouch. But at least that's some self-awareness. That has to count for something."

"Right." When they turned onto her street, he made eye contact with Daniel Riley and Bree Mallory. Hawkeye had operatives everywhere on the planet, but Trace knew both agents and was glad to see them assigned to the job. Mallory was competent and checked her ego at the door, making her great with high-maintenance clients. Riley was young, and during his short tenure, he'd volunteered for a lot of high-risk assignments. He'd already earned a big promotion.

Riley gave a slight nod, indicating everything was clear.

Aimee had been right about the length of the run. They arrived back at her house in just under fifty minutes. His heart rate was no longer in the danger zone, and he was finally able to draw a full breath. His protectee had set a grueling pace, especially given the terrain.

As she unlocked the door, he checked his phone to see a message from Lifeguard, their main contact at Hawkeye. The forensics crew had already finished their work.

"Aimee!" Eureka called. "Aimee! Aimee!"

"I'm back." Her hips swaying in a way he couldn't help but notice, Aimee crossed to the cage. "Let's get you out of there. Wait." She looked over her shoulder. "The team is done, right?"

For a second, he considered fibbing so that she'd leave Eureka in the cage.

Waiting, she drew her eyebrows together.

"Yeah. They have."

Focusing on her feathered friend, she opened the door for him to climb out. More agile than Trace could imagine, the feathered terror pulled himself to the top of the cage, then glared at Trace.

He kept a wary eye on the bird. And it was mutual. When Trace moved, the bird tracked him.

In the living room, Aimee bent over in a long, slow stretch.

His damnable heart rate slammed back into double time. He strode to the kitchen for a bottle of cold water and drained half of it in a single gulp.

This might turn out to be one of his more challenging assignments. He'd protected beautiful women before. But none of them had this kind of sensual effect on him.

She stood, reached for the ceiling, then eased slowly back, elongating her torso, displaying her toned body to perfection.

He finished the water and looked out the window so he didn't give in to the temptation to drag her against him, wrap her in his arms, then kiss her senseless. It was going to take every bit of his self-control to keep his hands off his boss's little sister.

CHAPTER THREE

HAWKEYE

W hen was imprisonment going to end?

The past three weeks had been the longest of Aimee's life.

Restless, she paced the length of her back patio, unable to look away from the six-foot privacy fence Trace had insisted she needed. Now, she couldn't enjoy the neighbor's flower garden with its colorful snapdragons and large pots filled with stunning lavender.

Ever since the break-in, her life had been turned upside down, taking her emotional equilibrium with it. Trace was everywhere, sleeping on her couch, cooking in her kitchen, showering in her guest bathroom, running on the treadmill in her office. He'd dealt with the forensics team that had gone through every bit of her house, overseen the technicians who'd installed the security system and set up monitoring in her office, authorized IT people to examine her computer for a hardware hack. Annoying her, he'd also started to make friends with Eureka. How was she supposed to dislike Trace when she'd caught him giving her bird a strawberry?

But maybe worst of all was the way she noticed the sexy agent. This morning, she'd been up early to work on her project.

She'd tiptoed toward the kitchen for coffee. Though she was as quiet as possible, Trace woke up. He tossed back the blanket and sat up. In a single move, he stood. Loose gray sweatpants rode low on his hips, showing his muscular abs and the tempting V-muscles near his groin.

Frozen in shock, she was still standing there when he rounded the couch, gun in hand. "Everything okay?"

When she didn't respond, he repeated the question.

"Ah." She cleared her throat. "Yes. I didn't mean to disturb you. Just up early. An idea I want to work on."

"Get up!" Eureka squawked. "Get up, get up, get up!"

"It appears we're all awake now," Trace replied, casting a glance at the birdcage.

"Sorry. I'll keep him in my bedroom from now on."

"No need. He's tolerable…at least sometimes." The words were begrudging but welcome. "How about I make the coffee and bring you a cup when it's ready?"

"Would you really?" With the craziness spinning inside her, she seized the opportunity to escape. With his sexy, sleepy eyes, the man was dangerous as hell. "Will you let Eureka out too?"

"Do I have to?"

"No." She smiled. "I'll do it while I make the coffee."

"Uhm." He placed his gun on the coffee table. "You go. I'll take care of the bird."

"Are you sure?" The previous day, she'd brewed the first pot. Since he dumped his cup down the drain when he obviously thought she wasn't watching, she could now put him in charge of coffee making and bird sitting.

"I got this."

Though she'd closed herself off from the living area of the

house, she hadn't been able to concentrate. While the machine gurgled and hissed, spitting out the aromatic brew, Trace was doing some type of exercise, if the sounds of his heavy breathing were anything to go by.

When he brought her a mug, a faded T-shirt clung to his chest, and a sexy sheen of sweat dotted his upper eyebrows.

Aimee wasn't sure she could take much more.

Pretending to be occupied with her work, when in reality she'd just minimized a cute otter video, she didn't look up as she murmured her gratitude.

Back in the dining room, she overheard him communicating with the team, ensuring everything was quiet. Then he took a shower.

He whistled, like he always did, and Eureka picked up a few notes as well, creating a cacophony of distraction.

At this rate, her part of the project would never be finished. And Trace would be assigned to her forever.

She pressed the heel of her palm against her forehead. Something had to change before she lost her mind.

Aimee sent a text message to her sister, and the response wasn't surprising.

UNTIL WE FIND OUT WHAT HAPPENED, TRACE STAYS.

AFTER SLAMMING DOWN THE PHONE HARDER THAN SHE intended, Aimee turned off her computer in favor of a long run on the treadmill. She set the speed ridiculously fast and ran hard, trying to shed the frustration. Twenty minutes later, out of breath and energy, she attempted to return to work.

Outside, rain began to splatter against the roof, matching her mood perfectly. And even with the door closed, the sound of the news on the television reached her, as did the deep, sensual tones of Trace's voice as he spoke on the phone.

Skies remained cloudy most of the day, adding to her inner tension. If she didn't get out soon, she was going to explode. With him around, she hadn't just lost her privacy, she had lost her concentration.

As the afternoon dragged on, the gray clouds began to dissipate, and she pulled her hair back into a ponytail and went into the backyard.

Now, still searching for some sort of peace, she dropped into a chair near the wrought-iron table.

What was wrong with her? Her focus had never been fractured like this before.

The door opened, and Trace exited the house. The late-afternoon sun played with strands of his hair, and as always, his musky, masculine scent aroused her.

"Is there any end in sight?" she asked as he took an uninvited seat across from her.

"Meaning?"

"You've been here for weeks." And nothing else had happened. No one else on the team had anything strange happen. Her files hadn't been hacked. "It had to have been a random thing. Kids or something."

"You'll have to take that up with your sister."

"I already tried." She needed her life to get back to normal. "I was hoping you could influence her."

"This assignment is fully at her discretion."

"Yeah. I know." Aimee blew out a breath. "It seems like a waste of resources." So many agents. In addition to Trace, there were two separate teams stationed in the neighborhood, providing twenty-four-hour coverage.

"Is it all bad?" He leaned toward her.

"You have to be losing your mind as well. Babysitting me can't be any fun for you."

"On the contrary. My cardiovascular capability has improved since I've started running with you. I can't keep up. Yet."

At his lighthearted comment, she couldn't help but grin. "You're a charming liar, Agent Romero, but a liar nonetheless. You'd rather be doing something much more exciting."

"Such as?" His gaze locked on her. Then slowly, he allowed it to drift over her.

Her pulse skidded to a halt. She'd imagined the sensual tone in his voice, hadn't she? She swallowed the sudden onslaught of nerves.

After his casual comment about seeing her collection of erotic books the first day he arrived, he hadn't mentioned it again. His search had been so thorough that she knew he had to have seen her toys. Had he wondered about them?

Aware of his scrutiny, she tried to remember his question. "Like, I don't know, battering down a door in some remote part of the planet."

"I don't know." He glanced up. "Denver in late summer isn't so bad. Better than a jungle somewhere."

Aimee pushed back from the table. "Well, enjoy it."

"Going somewhere?"

The sun had peeked out from behind the clouds, and she was seizing the opportunity. "I need a cocktail."

"I'll make you one. Margaritas are my specialty."

"No." She dragged the ponytail holder from her hair. "Just no. I'm going to take myself out to dinner and have the biggest rum cocktail I can find as I pretend I'm on a Caribbean beach somewhere."

"I'll be ready in fifteen minutes."

Had he listened to a single word? "What part of I'm taking myself out did you not understand?"

"You know the rules." He looked at her through his

impossibly long lashes, but there was nothing but lethal coldness in the depths of his brown eyes. "Don't push me, Miss Inamorata. You can't win, and you won't like my tactics."

Ever since she'd broken away from Jack, she'd hated bossy alpha men, and she'd never allowed another one to tell her what to do. "That sounds a bit like a threat."

"Doesn't have to be." He shrugged, but there was nothing casual about the motion. "You can consider it a gentle reminder or a friendly suggestion."

The words hung between them, as did his unveiled threat. She had no doubt he'd act on it. Her reaction was somewhere between petrified and intrigued. The last part bothered her the most.

"Do you have somewhere specific in mind?"

She tipped her head back. Though she rarely went out, not being able to jump in her car and go was maddening.

"Your choice. If there's somewhere you'd like to go, I'll make it happen."

Aimee sighed. He had, indeed, won. "There's a restaurant in Morrison that has a cool rooftop bar."

"What's the dress code?"

"Casual. There will be a lot of hikers, and some people dressed for a concert at Red Rocks, if there is one tonight."

"What's the name of the place?"

When she answered, he entered the information into his watch. "Team's notified. Fifteen minutes?" he asked, repeating his earlier question. "Or do you need longer?"

"The sooner the better."

Without another word, he went back inside, careful not to let Eureka out.

Confounding man.

Once she returned to her bedroom, Aimee changed into a short skirt while Trace closed the door to the bathroom and turned on the shower.

Even though he annoyed her, awareness of him blossomed.

It had to be natural. They were in close quarters with no other stimulation. Captives fell in love with captors. Survival of the species was hardwired into her.

She pulled on a tank top. Just because she understood the mechanics of their attraction didn't mean she wasn't woman enough to be firmly in its grasp.

When the shower fell silent, she slid into a pair of strappy sandals. As she walked past the closed bathroom door, the scent of his masculinity was imprinted on the air. And he was whistling.

Shaking her head, she continued to the dining room. Eureka was perched on the top of his cage, preening. "Step up." She put her hand in front of the bird. Instead of responding like he normally did, he walked away from her. "You don't have to go in for the night. I'll be right back."

Eureka shook his head.

"Having trouble?" Trace asked, joining her.

She turned to face him. His hair was damp, and his T-shirt was tight around his biceps and chest. He was devastatingly handsome, so much so that she suddenly couldn't breathe.

Ignoring him, she repeated her command to Eureka.

The parrot shook his head. "Aimee! Stay!"

"I'll be back. Promise."

Eureka lifted a foot to shield his face

"How about a walnut?" Trace offered.

The bribe would probably work. "Thank you."

Trace brought over the nut and placed it inside the cage, at the far corner. Still regarding them critically, Eureka went to explore the gift.

Once he was inside, she closed the door. "Most times he

doesn't mind going in his cage, but sometimes he can be stubborn."

"Not like anyone else I know." Trace cleared his throat, then smiled, disarming her.

His high-tech watch lit up with an alert. "Your car awaits."

"Ready?" He pulled on a formfitting black blazer that made him all the more impossibly handsome.

When she nodded, he pressed a key on his watch, and it was then that she noticed his tiny earpiece. "Falcon is ready to roll."

"What?" *Falcon?* "Why Falcon?"

"You like birds. And you're a flight risk."

"I don't want to be reminded that you're my keeper."

"Do you want to go or not?" He lifted a shoulder in a little uncaring shrug. "Your call."

Frustrated, she tucked a stray lock of hair behind her ear. "Yes."

In full secret agent man mode, he pulled back the drapes before offering her a tight nod.

Outside, a vehicle idled at the curb. As they approached, a woman exited to open the back door. "Afternoon, ma'am." The agent didn't smile.

Aimee scooted inside the SUV, and Trace slid in next to her, his thigh bumping into her. Senses swimming with awareness, she edged away from him.

"Agents Bree Mallory and Agent Daniel Riley." Trace introduced them as they pulled away from the curb.

Aimee crossed her legs, uncomfortable with the realization that her need to get out meant a lot of effort from the team. No matter how crazy she was going, the confinement wasn't just about her. Her actions impacted a number of people. "Thank you for doing this."

"It's a pleasure." Agent Riley met her gaze in the rearview mirror. "Turned out to be a beautiful afternoon."

In contrast to the dismal morning and drizzly noontime, now only a few high clouds danced across the cerulean sky.

Once they were away from the neighborhood and deeper into the rolling foothills, she relaxed against the seatback.

The tiny stress lines next to Trace's eyes were trenched in deeper than they had been this morning, reminding her of the sacrifice it was for him to escort her out in public.

Finally, in the heart of downtown Morrison, Agent Riley pulled to a stop in front of the restaurant, and Bree opened the door for them.

As if they were on a date, Trace offered his hand. Knowing it was anything but, she accepted, but when he held her tight, her stomach flip-flopped.

Though it wasn't necessary, he held her hand as they made their way up the wooden steps. When they reached the hostess station, he didn't let her go. Heat, as uncomfortable as it was unfamiliar, chased through her. It had been years since she'd reacted to a man in this way. Aimee gave herself a hard shake. Men like Trace were the reason she'd avoided dating.

Since it was still early, they had their selection of tables, and Trace chose one at the outer edge, close to an enormous cottonwood tree, shaded by an umbrella, and with a spectacular view.

The moment she sank into the chair that he held for her, her stress eased…until he scanned the occupants and angled himself so he could catalog every person walking into the bar.

"Could we pretend you're not my bodyguard?"

"We could." He grinned. "But I'm not going to."

"Look, Agent—"

"Trace," he corrected, maybe for the hundredth time. "At least for tonight. You'd call me Trace if I wasn't protecting you."

31

She met his eyes. They weren't filled with challenge as they had been earlier. In fact, they were inviting. She kept her distance because using his first name would be a step toward destroying the wall she needed to keep between them.

The server brought over two glasses of water, and Aimee ordered the sweet, fruity cocktail she'd promised herself.

"For you, sir?"

"I'm good with the water."

Less than five minutes later, the first sip of her punch flooded through her, warming her insides and chasing away the stress.

"How is it?"

"Lethal." Over the rim of the glass, she looked at him. "I forgot to order it without the rum shooter on top."

"Enjoy it."

She did. While Morrison wasn't the same as being on a Caribbean beach, the evening was pretty close to perfect. A gentle breeze drifted around them, and the sun trekked toward the foothills, turning the sky a spectacular shade of orange. "At times like this, I realize how much of a homebody I've become." She stirred her drink with the tiny red straw. "I should enjoy the sunset more. How about you"—she hesitated before opting to use just his last name—"Romero? Do you take time to notice the sky?"

"Sunrise? Sunset? No. The weather, yes. Rain, wind, temperature potentially impacts my work."

"The stars?"

"The full moon makes it easier to move at night." His eyes took on a faraway look, as if he was remembering some past event, reminding her they had so little in common.

The server arrived with their food. Aimee picked up a thick-cut French fry and took a bite. "So, how long have you done this secret-agent stuff?"

He grinned, relaxing for the first time since they'd left the house. "I wouldn't call it that."

"Okay." She popped a second fry into her mouth. "This never noticing the sunshine thing."

"All my life. Went to the police academy right out of school, like my dad. Like my older brother. Most of my uncles. Eventually, I was bored, so I tried out for the SWAT team."

"You like risk."

"Being challenged. If I had it to do over again, I might join the military instead. Try out for Special Ops."

"How did you learn about Hawkeye?"

"Through a friend. Nate Davidson. Do you know him?"

She shook her head. "I've heard of him, though."

"Working for Hawkeye is more interesting than police work. I never know what I'm going to be doing, where I'll be sent. I volunteer for extra assignments."

"The riskier the better?"

"You could say that."

She leaned toward him a little. "Where's home?"

"Wherever I am."

"So no permanent address?" So different from how she lived her life. Because of her father's chronic unemployment, her parents had moved a lot, and then after they died, Aimee and her sister had rented a two-bedroom apartment in the Denver suburbs. Even that had proved costly, so they'd downsized again. During college, she'd shared with three roommates. As soon as Aimee fled from Jack, she'd bought her small home and cocooned herself in it.

"No. Most of my family lives in Texas, near Dallas. I visit when I can."

"You still have your parents?"

"I do. Both of them. Mom's always run the house, and Dad recently retired. I think he's driving her a little crazy."

The affection in his tone made Aimee smile. She was thirteen when she'd lost her mom and dad. She'd been in a rebellious period, thinking her parents were trying to restrict the freedom she wanted, and she recalled some loud arguments. If she could have known the horrible gulf looming before her when they'd been hit head-on during a storm... Growing up without that anchor left a hole in her heart that she'd never been able to fill, even though she'd tried, with Jack. "You're fortunate."

"I think so. Until Mom asks when I'm going to settle down and give her grandbabies. I'm grateful for my sister who's getting ready to have her first. My mother moved in with her temporarily so she doesn't miss a single thing. She was afraid they'd go to the hospital and not tell her. Said she didn't want to see the first pictures of her new grandchild on social media." He grinned. "My brother-in-law is beyond unhappy about that. He appealed to my dad for help, but all of them are helpless against the force that is my mom. At any rate, Deanna has taken the pressure off the rest of us, for the moment, at least."

"The rest of you? How many siblings do you have?"

"I'm one of six. Four boys, two girls. I'm right in the middle. My oldest brother is considering a run for mayor."

"Impressive." For as long as she could remember, it had just been her and her sister, struggling to stay together and survive.

Trace plucked a fry from the oversize basket between them.

"I'm shocked to see you eat that." At her house, he'd cooked most of his own food, a ridiculous number of salads and lean meats.

"You might be shocked at the number of things I like."

She swallowed hard, unaccountably, again, recalling his comment the first day about her reading material. "I'm sure some of them are dangerous." Her question had to be the result of the rum.

"In the mind of the beholder, I suppose."

Aimee stirred the remnants of her drink.

"I prefer to think of them as enthralling."

She glanced away.

"And you, Miss Inamorata? Burgers and fries don't seem to fit your personality, either. Soy lattes. Fresh veggies."

If she didn't have the courage, and a touch of bravado, from the cocktail, she might have kept her mouth shut. Instead, she replied in kind. "Like you said, you might be shocked at the number of things I like."

"Would I?" He took a drink of his water. "Try me out."

The words—the temptation—hung between them. He captured her gaze, and her heart galloped. She wanted to be bold, but suddenly she couldn't string words together in the right order.

The server returned, and Aimee boldly opted for a second cocktail. For courage, maybe? "And a piece of key lime pie." If she was going to be reckless, she might as well go all the way.

"Two forks," Trace said, surprising her again.

After dinner, she asked if they could stroll down Bear Creek Avenue. After informing the team, he nodded.

"I'm sure it's your favorite thing."

"You know, Miss Inamorata, protecting you isn't all bad."

She furrowed her eyebrows as she looked at him, searching for any hint that he wasn't telling the truth.

He took care of the bill, then helped her from her chair.

"Are you always such a gentleman?"

"Part of the service." His smile was quick, genuine, and it did funny things to her pulse.

As they meandered to a shop, he placed his fingers in the small of her back, and she jumped as if electricity had arced through her.

Her attraction to him was as real as it was dangerous. She needed to rein in her hormones. He wasn't a friend or lover. He was a man well paid to be with her. Forgetting that would be stupid.

Still, he was aware and attentive as she browsed through a gallery, then a curio shop.

Finally, she purchased half a pound of homemade fudge in a rustic-looking store.

The Hawkeye SUV idled out front, and she'd been aware of Mallory and Riley never letting her out of their sights. It was overkill, she was sure. But she'd never convince her sister of that. Still, it was better than staying in the house again. "Thank you for this evening."

"I've enjoyed it."

"Have you?" She broke off a piece of the chocolate peanut butter confection and offered it to him.

"The pie was enough for me."

After one bite of her second dessert, she was inclined to agree with him. "We should get the rest of the team some burgers."

"That's thoughtful of you. I'm sure that would be appreciated."

After walking up and down the aisles of the last store that was still open, they returned to the restaurant to place a to-go order.

Twenty minutes later, they were back in the car and on the way home.

"Much appreciated, ma'am," Riley said when she handed over the bag filled with food.

"I love fries," Mallory added. "My weakness."

"How about some fudge too?" Aimee offered that bag to Mallory, also. "I'm afraid my sweet tooth got the better of me. And I don't want to run for three hours tomorrow to work it off."

"I don't want you to have to do that either," Trace added drily.

"Thank you. I'm not a fan, though. How about you, Riley? You'll eat anything."

"Oh, yeah. Definitely."

Mallory accepted the gift and placed it on the console near Riley. "This will get me through the rest of the shift," he said, meeting her gaze in the rearview mirror with a quick smile. "Thanks."

"Thank you for saving me from myself. Oh, and it's not Donna, Ruth, or Julie."

"Ma'am?" Mallory asked, turning slightly in his seat.

"My sister's first name." Aimee smiled. "I understand there's quite a pool of money available to the person who figures out her name."

"Enough to take a nice trip to the Virgin Islands."

"Or put a down payment on a house," Riley added.

"Not that we're interested in obtaining inside information, ma'am," she amended hastily.

"And it's not Louise."

Mallory was grinning as she turned back around.

The conversation ended, and Aimee's unease crept back in. The outing should have refreshed her. Instead, sitting next to Trace as they navigated through traffic bothered her. His knee touched hers. Heat flared, reigniting the same reaction she'd had earlier when he commandingly put his fingers against her. He glanced at her, and even in the darkness, his intensity slid through her.

She should move away, but she didn't.

Neither did he.

When they turned a corner, they came in even greater contact, and he placed his hand on her leg to steady her.

She pulled away, as if scalded.

Every glance, holding hands, sharing dessert, laughing

together, had ratcheted up her awareness of him until she wanted to crawl out of her skin.

Or worse, quench the craving.

When the vehicle stopped in front of her home, she hurried out, rather than waiting for one of the agents.

Trace rounded the vehicle and jogged to catch up with her. When she fumbled with the lock, he took the key from her. "I can do this," she protested.

"Of course you can." He covered her hand with his. "But you're going to let me." He stood impossibly close, using his body to shield hers, reminding her she was his client, and nothing more.

Telling herself, again, that she couldn't afford any ridiculous sort of notions about him, she sighed.

When he finally released the lock, she hurried inside.

"Aimee!" Eureka called, desperately, she imagined.

While Trace secured the door, she went to say hello to her pet, grateful, more than ever, for the distraction.

"Out. Out, out, out."

"I know. I promised." She offered her hand, and he climbed on.

"Whee!"

She carried Eureka to the perch she'd set up for him in her office. After misting him with a water bottle so that he could occupy himself by preening, she forced away her disturbing thoughts about Trace and her damn strong feminine reaction to him. Hoping she could focus, Aimee powered up her computer and logged in to the group discussion board for her work project.

The most recent update was a video from Jason Knoll, a young, brilliant computer prodigy. As a fourteen-year-old, he'd written a game that had been purchased by one of the world's largest producers of video games, making him a millionaire. Today, he wore an in-your-face yellow T-shirt, had long uncombed hair, walked around in bare feet, and every motion was animated to the point of exaggeration.

They'd been on the same team for over a year, working to develop a state-of-the-art way to spy on people, by utilizing devices that resembled insects.

The evening before, he'd launched one that looked like a mosquito. The video showed the bug moving through the air. She cheered when it successfully navigated away from a hanging bug zapper. That was an amazing bit of programming work. But then, a neighbor picked up a can of insect repellant and sprayed the mosquito. She gasped in horror as the expensive insect wobbled then plunged to the grass.

"We took a lot of things into consideration," Jason said. "But not that. Stuff is sticky as hell. If anyone has any ideas, let me know."

The video ended.

She was working on the injection part of the project, and she had her own set of challenges. About five percent of the time, her delivery mechanism didn't work as designed. When the stakes were high, that failure rate wasn't acceptable. She opened up her code to take a fresh look at it.

In the quiet, she couldn't ignore Trace's sounds as he checked the doors and windows, even though the house had been under surveillance the entire time they were gone. As if that wasn't enough, the surveillance video was streamed to Hawkeye headquarters as well as all members of the team.

Fort Knox had less security.

He entered the office, and Eureka called out, "Agent!"

She scowled. Disloyal avian, greeting her nemesis.

"Hey, you green menace."

As if he'd understood every word, Eureka lifted a leg.

She looked back at her screen to hide her grin.

After ensuring the window was latched, Trace left her alone, and she exhaled in relief. She never remembered a time when her attraction for a man eclipsed her interests in work.

The sound of his voice as he spoke on the phone to Riley reassured her, and simultaneously reminded her of the intimacy he'd shown at dinner.

A little while later, the word *Madre* drifted toward her, and he asked about his expectant sister.

An hour later, her eyes tired from looking at code that she couldn't decipher, she sighed and admitted defeat before pushing back from her workspace.

Eureka turned toward her, and she placed her hand near him. "Step up. Time for bed." It didn't surprise her that he chose to be naughty and move to the far end of the perch. She shouldn't have told him he was going to bed. "Step up," she repeated, moving her hand closer to him.

For a moment, he ignored her command. "Eureka," she coaxed.

After a few more seconds, he relented.

"Good bird."

"Good bird," he repeated. "Good bird. Good bird."

She carried him back to the dining room to settle in for the night. Trace was in the kitchen, uncapping a bottle of water. The house was quiet, and her insides were suddenly a livewire of tension.

"Look, Aimee, about what happened—"

"Thanks for taking me out tonight." She needed to excuse herself, make a mad dash for the bedroom. Instead, she remained where she was.

Trace placed his drink on the counter. "Come here."

Every instinct for preservation flashed with warning. But something more urgent—feminine to masculine—responded to his quiet command. Obediently, she moved a couple of steps closer.

He took her shoulders in a firm but loose grip. If she tried to pull away, she knew he'd let her go. "Taking this any further might be a hell of a mistake."

"I know." She swallowed, but she was lost in his eyes. Raw desire was there, in the rich, deep depths.

"I want to kiss you. Tell me no."

For a million reasons, she should run. Instead, she shook her head. "I… Yes."

He moved one hand to the back of her head, then inched up and spread his fingers to fist her hair.

Trace was as forceful as he was commanding, and it was the illicit thrill she knew it would be.

"Preciosa."

With purpose, he held her captive and moved toward her.

He brushed his soft, sensual lips across hers, as if giving her a taste, but also one last chance to run away.

She swayed toward him.

"So perfect." He kissed her, seeking entrance to her mouth.

With a soft sigh, she surrendered. At first his tongue was seeking, as if he wanted to learn the secret to her responses. When she lifted onto her toes, he plundered deeper, taking what she offered, then asking for more.

He tasted of seduction. Of temptation. And his scent was spice and chilled alpine air, as untamed as he was.

Far too soon, he began to withdraw. He was no longer dominant. In fact, he was tender, easing his grip to make small circles with his fingertips, massaging away the tiny ache he'd caused.

He left her breathless.

Slowly, he released her shoulder, then tucked wild strands of hair back behind her ear with a gentleness that captivated her. "I'm sending you to bed, querida. Before I can't."

"Yes." They were sliding toward something that might destroy her emotionally. Keeping her distance was smart, even if her body ached with demand. "Good night." She turned away. Though she didn't look back, heat from his gaze followed her down the hall.

At the bedroom door, she paused. Unable to stop herself, she turned.

He was there, arms folded. Uninviting.

Hoping he was as frustrated as she was, Aimee went inside and closed the door. Alone, she pressed her fingers to her mouth, as she tried to pretend it had meant nothing to her.

In the living room, the television blared to life, and Eureka squawked in protest until Trace turned down the volume.

She changed into nightclothes, then, for more than an hour, her thoughts in riot, she tossed and turned.

Eventually the house fell quiet, the sudden silence seeming to echo. She tuned in to the sound of water running in the kitchen, then quiet again before Trace said a few words, presumably on the phone, but he could have been talking to Eureka since the parrot said something that could have been "Night-night."

Trace's footfall was firm on the hardwood floor as he made his nightly rounds, through the office, then back down the hallway.

She held her breath, fearing he'd knock, hoping he would.

Though the movements she could discern became fainter, she imagined him pulling off his shirt, then changing into his thin, reveal-damn-near everything sleep pants.

The kiss had devastated her. He'd awakened a physical reaction. More frighteningly, he'd evoked her emotions. She hungered for him, while knowing she dare not go any further.

Aimee punched her pillow into shape, but she still couldn't drift off. Taking a bath to relax might wake him up, but she needed to do something to escape the turmoil rolling inside her.

Careful to not make too much noise, she turned on the lamp, then slipped from the bed to grab a book. Instead of picking up a scholarly read or even a mystery, she allowed her fingers to hover over her more erotic titles.

With a sigh, she selected an anthology with short and intensely hot vignettes, some Victorian in nature, one a medieval historical, another a contemporary fantasy. But in all of them, she was the heroine, and Trace was the hero. In this particular one, she was a princess who needed taming, and he was the duke, dressed in fashionable breeches and polished boots, impatiently tapping a cane against his calf.

She tossed aside the book and rolled to her stomach, working her hand beneath her to finger her clit.

The angle didn't quite work for her, and in frustration, she turned back over, then went to grab the vibrator from the bottom drawer. No doubt Trace had seen it, along with her other toys. At least he'd had the courtesy not to mention what he'd found.

She buried herself beneath the covers to dull the sound of her toy before sliding it on to the lowest setting.

Rather than satisfying her, the tiny fluttering annoyed her. She needed more.

She closed her eyes and spread her pussy before turning the device to a higher speed.

Unbidden, thoughts of Trace danced through her mind. But instead of one of the short stories she'd just read, she imagined them being alone, with him directing her what to do, giving her a spanking—her first—and encouraging her to learn what she liked. He'd be unrelenting and determined, his voice gruff, granting her no reprieve.

The orgasm loomed just out of reach. But when she

pictured Trace guiding her hand, she cried out, shaking, breathless as she came.

Somehow she managed to turn off the vibrator before she dropped it beside her.

That had been the most powerful climax she'd had in months.

What would sex with Trace be like? Romantic? Maybe frenetic because their relationship would end the moment he was reassigned?

She sighed. Was he even a Dom? She didn't even know that much. His interest in her reading material might have been passing.

Aimee pushed wayward strands of hair back from her forehead. Even if he was, it didn't matter. Though Hawkeye didn't have a strict policy against fraternization, getting involved with a teammate was a bad idea—particularly a protective agent who was as demanding and bossy as Trace Romero. If getting involved was a bad idea, then getting spanked by him would be stupendously stupid.

So why couldn't she stop thinking about it?

CHAPTER FOUR

HAWKEYE

Aimee's soft moans drifted through the house, making Trace's cock already harder than it had been after their kiss.

Jesus.

To focus on something other than what she was doing behind the closed door, he recited the alphabet backward.

Fuck.

The fact that she was masturbating drove him mad. Protecting the professor's seriously hot body had just become one of his most difficult assignments ever. He'd never been this attracted to a client.

If they'd met under different circumstances, he might want to introduce her to BDSM. Then again, maybe not.

He tossed back the sheet and dropped to the floor to do push-ups.

The women he scened with knew the score. They were experienced players and had similar no-strings-attached expectations. They liked the thrill as much as he did.

But Aimee, despite her blasé attitude, was an innocent.

Since he made it a point not to play with anyone new,

that shouldn't appeal to him. But fuck if he didn't want to be the man to introduce her to her more primal desires.

Trace continued to push himself until his arms shook from the exertion. He had no idea how many push-ups he'd done. Counting wasn't the point. Forgetting how sweet Aimee's mouth had tasted was.

Finally, she cried out with a slight whimper. She'd climaxed, which should allow him to shove thoughts of her aside so he could go to sleep.

Should.

He continued to drive himself to fatigue. His form sucked, which meant he needed to stop.

Trace returned to the couch and couldn't settle. Too damn hot, and the couch wasn't long enough. Until tonight, that hadn't been a complaint. Through his career, he'd slept in a whole lot worse places—dirt floors, craggy mountains, blanket rolls, camping cots.

After checking the house again, he opted for a quick shower.

The cool Colorado water gushing over him did nothing to diminish his raging erection. And thoughts of what Aimee must have looked like as she slid her fingers—or was it a toy?—across her clit tormented him. He ached to be inside her.

Recalling her sensual moans, he took his cock in hand and stroked up and down, pulling hard, picturing her beneath him. He wanted her whimpers filling his ears. Wanted to devour her cries with his hungry mouth.

In spite of the millions of reasons he needed to think about anything other than Aimee, he closed his eyes and stroked harder.

Then, consumed by her, he ejaculated in long ribbons, her name on his tongue, her image seared into his brain.

With a shake of his head, as if that would clear his mind,

Trace rinsed off. Then he toweled dry with more force than necessary.

He pulled on his sleep pants and tugged a T-shirt on. Jacking off hadn't helped. In fact, it had the opposite effect. Knowing she was next door, all snug in bed, made his dick swell again.

Before leaving the bathroom, Trace raked a hand through his short, damp hair.

Aimee's door stood ajar. With a frown, he returned to the living room.

"Couldn't sleep," she confessed, standing in the living room. A sleep shirt covered her to midthigh, but his imagination filled in the rest.

"You need to go back to bed." His voice was rough, cut with warning.

"I know." Yet she stayed where she was, smelling of seduction. "I…uhm…"

He waited.

"About my reading material." Her expressive blue eyes drew him in. She was all feminine sensuality and softness, awakening the predator inside him.

"Aimee, I'm here for your safety." This moment, she needed to protect herself from him.

She nodded. "I'm curious. About BDSM."

Sweet Jesus.

"I mean, from a scholarly perspective. I may want to write an academic paper."

"An academic paper?"

"Okay. No. That was a lie. A white one, but still. I'm interested because… Well, I've wondered. And I have a few questions."

"And you think I'm the right person to ask?"

"Uh… Did I misunderstand? Do you…?" She flushed.

"Look." What the hell should he say next? Hoping he

wasn't walking into quicksand, he answered her. "Yeah. I have a fair amount of experience." He searched her face. "The only thing you want to do is talk?"

"That's a good place to start." She tipped her head back to meet his gaze. "Right?"

Her hair was tousled, maybe from the way her head had moved against the pillow as she'd pleasured herself. "Could you put a robe on?"

"I thought…" She blinked and looked down at herself. "This is long. Longish, anyway."

"You're not nearly covered enough." A low, menacing growl undercut his voice.

Still, she hesitated.

Trace spoke again, and this time, there was warning mixed with a command. "Go and change, Aimee. Right now."

Like the smart woman she was, she went back to her room. Foolishly, perhaps, she returned.

Thank God, she was encased in a floor-length robe. Not that it made any difference. "We'll sit in the dining room."

Her eyebrows furrowed in that quizzical way he'd come to expect from her. It wasn't necessarily an argument, but something didn't make sense to her logical, professorial mind. "The couch is more comfortable."

Making it far too easy for her to scoot close to him. "I prefer the table." Instead of arguing, he crossed to the dining room and pulled out a chair for her.

Eureka blinked at them, then closed his eyes again.

"I'll make tea."

"You sure caffeine is a good choice?"

"Chamomile. It's herbal. Soothing."

He took a seat and watched her fill the electric kettle.

"Can I brew you a cup?"

If it would take away his tension, maybe he should ask for a gallon. Instead, he shook his head.

While the water heated, she took down a tiny cup and matching saucer. No way would his finger fit through the little curlicue handle.

She sat across from him. "Are you a Dom?"

"What's your understanding of what that means?"

Smoothing back her enticing, mussed hair, Aimee sighed. "You're supposed to be answering the questions."

"Sorry." He gave a halfhearted grin. Her frustration wasn't funny. "This isn't a college lecture. There will be nothing academic about this discussion."

"Well, most of my reading has been fiction, but…" She cleared her throat. "Well, you looked at my bookcase. You know I've got a couple of manuals that a friend of mine recommended."

"Go on."

"I've read about safe, sane, consensual play. And safe words."

"You have done your research." Of course she had. "Good."

She squirmed. "This is making me uncomfortable."

"It's your choice of whether to go on or not." He preferred she didn't.

"No. I mean, I want to know, and it's the only way I'll find out. Right?"

He shrugged.

The kettle shrilled. As if being given a reprieve, she jumped up.

He tracked her as she turned off the heat. Her hand shook as she dumped a tea bag in the cup, then added the hot water.

She carried it back, then took her seat again. Staring into the depths of the cup, she continued. "I know that some people are masochists and others are sadists. Which can be impact play or more than that, right?"

"Please look at me."

Twin scarlet streaks were painted on her cheekbones. Sweet and tempting.

She cleared her throat and sat up, perhaps like she might in the classroom. "There's a lot to it. A lot of different kinks, and I guess no two people do it the same."

"Agreed."

"For example, some people like light bondage, maybe handcuffs and nothing else. Or blindfolds." She cleared her throat. "Subs. Slaves. Bottoms. Tops. Masters." She paused. "Owners. It can be a little confusing." Her tone was a little distant, as if she wasn't talking about herself. "My friend and her husband limit scenes to the weekend, and she knows other couples who keep it in the bedroom only. She tells me a number of people just like to go to clubs—or dungeons. I've also heard about submissives who are into it because they enjoy the service parts of it."

"Which applies to you?"

"To…" She pulled the lapels of her robe closer. "Me?"

"Not some hypothetical couple. You, Aimee. When you read, I'm sure you're drawn to certain things. In your fantasies, what do you like?"

"A lot of different things. I do know that a full-time thing wouldn't work for me, although…" She picked up the string of her tea bag and dragged it from side to side in a figure-eight motion. When she met his gaze again, her eyes were wide. "I have to confess that I read a fair amount of those kinds of stories."

"What did you choose earlier this evening?"

"How did you know—"

"I heard you."

"Oh." She dropped the string. "I'm going to die. I think I'm going to die."

"Nothing to be embarrassed about, especially in light of what we're talking about. BDSM is about honesty. It's about trust. You have to be able to tell me anything. And more, you have to face who you are and what you want. Not that you can't—or won't—change and evolve, but you'll never get your needs met unless you're able to look them in the face and share them, if not with me, then someone else." On the final word, he clenched his back teeth. Suddenly, he had no intention of letting any other man near her. "You're safe with me, Aimee. Your body, your mind, your limits. I know it's hard to admit certain things, but getting what you want comes with risk."

She pulled out the tea bag and placed it on the saucer. "I was reading a short story. About a duke and a princess."

"He was the Dom?"

"Oh. Yes. Of course."

"Just checking that she—and by extension, you—were not the Domme."

"No." She shook her head in denial. "Absolutely not."

"Tell me more about it."

"Well, it was kind of a *Taming of the Shrew* kind of story. He married her, but she didn't behave like a proper princess."

He nodded. "So he used corporal punishment?"

She took a sip of her drink, then took her time swallowing it. "A crop."

"What kind of experience do you have?"

"None."

"By none, you mean…what, exactly?"

"I have never had a scene."

His cock rose demandingly. He did his damn best to ignore it. "No boyfriend, date, has ever tied you up?"

She shook her head.

"Spanking? Even playful?"

Her eyes took on a faraway look. "No." Pain wove through her admission, and he ached to soothe it away.

He'd been with plenty of masochists and subs, and he'd

never probed this deep before. They met, discussed their various kinks and safe words, then made an agreement or wished each other a polite good evening. Aimee was different, and it wasn't just because he was assigned to her. He wanted to get to know her. "But you've wanted to?"

"I had a serious relationship, and I hoped that maybe one day…" She moved the bottom of the cup in little circles in the saucer's indentation. "I didn't trust him."

"He was a boyfriend?" She didn't need to answer, but he wondered if she would.

"It was more serious than that. Thankfully I managed to get out before the wedding. I'm not sure what would have happened if I had ever given him that kind of power."

Yet she was talking to him. Fuck if that didn't make him happy. Stupidly so.

"But I asked about you. If you were a Dom."

"As you said yourself, it's complicated. A Top, for sure. That can be used interchangeably with Dom in some people's eyes."

"You told me—when we had our first run—that you had a girlfriend. Was BDSM part of that?" She abandoned the cup in favor of looking at him.

"Yeah. For a time. She and I had different views on what that meant, and neither of our jobs were conducive for sorting that out. We didn't have long stretches of time to talk about it. I was on the SWAT team and would get called away. And she was a cop too. Then she joined the military. She shipped out to basic training less than twenty-four hours after telling me. She kept it secret for who knows how long. Days? Weeks?" He shrugged, even though there was nothing casual about it to him. It had fucking hurt. He'd failed, and it still bothered him.

"Was it part of any other relationship?"

"No. And I'll be honest with you, Aimee—I've never

considered it again. If the experience taught me anything, it's that my job is better suited to less formal arrangements, so I keep it that way."

"That makes sense, I suppose. But I don't really understand what that means."

"I don't make promises I can't keep. I enjoy my kink at clubs or parties, where the players understand and agree to the rules and everyone has been vetted. No strings. I don't know what drove Monica to leave in that way. But the ending is a regret I carry."

"A good relationship takes two people being fully committed and working hard, Trace." Her tone was soft, rounded by sympathy. "It can't be all your fault."

He appreciated Aimee's fierce loyalty, and she cracked open a part of his heart he'd long since walled over. "Thank you."

"I mean it."

"Any more questions? Or should I send you back to bed?"

He watched her draw her eyebrows together as she contemplated his question, no doubt weighing what was best against her natural curiosity.

"I'm curious about the psychological parts of it." She looked at him. "From what I've heard, and read, it's a bit of a mind fuck."

"Subspace, potentially. An endorphin rush." He shrugged. "Experiencing new things. Pushing boundaries. Surrendering to someone else."

"It's a lot."

"Yeah."

"I should go to bed."

"Yeah. You should." *Before I can't let you go.*

She stood, slowly. Reluctantly, he wanted to believe. Then she crossed her arms over her chest and clutched her robe's lapels. "Good night."

He tracked her movements down the hall, noted her hesitation before she gently closed her bedroom door.

Trace stayed where he was for a while. He should be relieved. Instead, regret pounded through him, hard and relentless.

"I'D LIKE TO GO FOR A RUN." AIMEE BREEZED INTO THE kitchen to grab a protein bar from the cupboard. As she tore open the wrapper, she tried not to breathe in Trace's power or scent.

It was still early, right before dawn, and she hadn't slept more than a couple of hours.

Trace didn't seem to be faring much better. He stood in front of the coffee maker, waiting for the miserly thing to give up its first cup. "Now?" Judging by the fact that he was still in his sleep pants and that he hadn't shaven, he hadn't gotten any more rest than she had. A tiny part of her was glad that last night had bothered him.

She'd spent the night alternating between tormented dreams and lucid fantasies. It was nearly dawn when she fell into a fitful sleep. Aimee wished she'd been strong enough not to run. But his comment about surrender had ricocheted in her head, and for a moment, old fears—of Jack—had returned. Since him, she'd kept her guard up, trusting no man.

Aimee had enough self-awareness to recognize that the two men couldn't be compared. Trace had ten times more restraint than her ex. But still, he was a dominant, bossy alpha male. And turning over her body and mind to him, with only a safe word as a lifeline, was an enormous risk.

Though nervous energy streaked through her, urging her out the door immediately, it was still dark out, and he deserved at least one cup of coffee. "Will twenty minutes be okay?"

"Yeah. Should be fine." He poured a cup of coffee, took a gulp that must have burned his mouth, then went to the living room, grabbed his duffel bag from beneath the end table, unzipped it to pull out running clothes. He paused to look at her. "Don't think about going alone."

Because of the energy gnawing at her, it had been a consideration. "I know better." But that would make the whole team scramble, and that wasn't fair.

With a tight nod, he headed for the bathroom.

"Aimee! Out! Out, out, out!"

She exhaled a breath she hadn't realized she'd been holding.

After putting her uneaten breakfast back on the counter, she opened Eureka's cage and placed her hand inside. "Step up."

"Whee!" He soared into flight and stole her protein bar.

Since it was too heavy, he ended up dropping it. "Now neither of us get to eat it," she said.

He cruised back to his cage and perched on the top. "Pretty bird."

"Uh-huh." She got him a walnut, since it had been effective for Trace, and placed it inside the cage.

When he went to grab it, she closed the cage again.

"I need to go for a run. I'll let you out again when I get back."

Trace turned on the shower, and her thoughts once again returned to the previous evening. What would have happened if she hadn't run? Sex? A spanking? Nothing?

That wasn't an option. After his kiss, and then refusing to be alone with her until she'd dressed in a full-length robe, she'd known he was as interested in her as she was him.

Trace joined her, his hair damp, smelling of spicy soap.

"Let me check in with the team first." He touched a button on his high-tech watch. "Falcon wants to go for a run."

"She going to leave you in the dust again, Romero?"

She grinned. Sounded like Riley.

"You're welcome to take my place."

Silence returned, and she exchanged grins with Trace.

Intimacy. How had it happened? When had it happened? Slowly, over the time they'd shared, the weeks of watching television, sharing meals, taking care of Eureka, sleeping beneath the same roof.

At times, like yesterday, it still chafed. Occasionally, she liked it.

"Come back," Riley said, some seconds later. "We have a bad connection, Romero."

"Two minutes," Trace said. "I'm hoping she takes pity and allows us to run on the track."

"I'd rather do the trail," she replied.

"Your lucky day, Romero." Riley's voice was ridiculously cheerful.

About sixty seconds later, his voice again filled the living room. "All clear. Martin is heading over there now."

She frowned, glancing up from her fitness watch. Though it made sense, she hadn't realized another agent ran with them.

"Joseph Martin?" Trace asked.

"Yeah. He's back on duty."

"Good to hear." Trace glanced at her. "You ready?"

She tightened her ponytail. "I am now."

Because she was tired and groggier than she would ever admit, she set a reasonable pace, and Trace didn't have to work as hard as normal to keep up. He'd done better every day as he acclimated. "Who's Joseph Martin?" she asked as they reached the end of the street.

"A fellow agent. He was shot while protecting Wolf Stone."

She'd heard stories about the legendary Stone, and knew that there'd been a huge bounty on his head, to prevent him from testifying in a high-profile court case. "I'm glad he's okay."

"So am I. For a long time, we weren't sure he'd ever be fit for duty again."

The trail was single track, which meant they couldn't talk once they started the ascent. Maybe that was the reason she'd chosen Green Mountain rather than opting for the high school where he could remain by her side.

She kept her heart rate where she wanted it and reached the end of the trail. Trace was right behind her, barely winded. "Nice job, Romero." With a grin, she headed back down the mountain.

At the end, she slowed to a walk. Now that she had some energy, she wanted to talk, and it was easier outside than in the confines of her house. "I thought we might walk back."

"You're showing mercy? Now?" he asked.

"I didn't sleep well." She shrugged, as if the admission hadn't cost her much.

"You want to tell me about it?"

Grasping for courage, she nodded.

He fell in step next to her. "I'm all ears."

"I want to know why you got into BDSM."

"Does your mind ever stop?"

She slid him a glance. There was no judgment in his voice, but rather, genuine interest. "Honestly? I'm trying to make sense of the whole thing."

"You know, Miss Inamorata, you keep wading into very hazardous waters."

Yet she couldn't stay away.

A minute later, when she wasn't sure whether or not he

would respond, he spoke. "There was a guy at the police academy who belonged to an exclusive club in New Orleans. The Quarter. We drove down for a few days after graduation and visited the dungeon. I didn't participate, but it wasn't anything like I expected. I guess at the base level, it was the same thing that drew me to police work. The thrill."

"And you already had the handcuffs." She shouldn't have said that, provocative, flirting in a way.

"I already had the handcuffs," he agreed. "I joined a club in Dallas. Had to go through some classes first, and I was assigned a mentor. Learned the ropes. So to speak."

It was his turn to tease, and butterflies of awareness danced in her.

"I like the implements, how they each do different things to a woman's body. And pleasing a submissive is the most sublime of experiences. There's a rush I don't get anywhere else. We might be in a room filled with people, dozens of scenes going on, but no one but her exists. I'm focused—maybe in the same way I am right before I deploy into a dangerous situation. Her responses become my world."

Was it really that way for a Dom. She drew her eyebrows together.

"What?"

They turned onto her street and passed the SUV that Riley and Bree Mallory occupied. Bree, always reserved, surprised her by lifting her coffee cup in salute as they walked by.

"I think she likes that you kick my ass."

She grinned. "Since it's probably the only thing I'll ever win at, I'm going to celebrate my victory."

They put their conversation on hold until they returned to the house. As usual, the ever-vigilant Trace locked the door, then checked all the windows, then each room, before disappearing into the office, no doubt to check the surveillance video.

She opened the cage for Eureka. Trace nudged her aside as she pulled down a bag of coffee from the cupboard. She scowled. He'd turned off the switch before they left, and the remnants in the carafe were cold. He might be tough enough to drink a warmed up cup, but she wasn't.

"I'll do it. You can, ah, relax. Relaxing is good."

Eureka flew over and perched on the top of the refrigerator to watch him, and no doubt to secure more food of his own.

"How about I make you an omelet?" Trace offered.

The contents of the fridge were a little bare since they hadn't been to the grocery store recently. She'd spent her days working, her evenings thinking about Trace. "That would be great. Thanks."

"We should call the supermarket and have them deliver some food later."

"I'd rather go myself." When he raised his right eyebrow, she sighed. "Right. We'll go together." Along with half of the Hawkeye team. "We can combine it with my coffee run." That would save them deploying another two times. The logistics of getting through the day unnerved her.

"Uhm, I need to get eggs from the refrigerator." He eyed Eureka.

"Off there," she told the bird, putting her hand in front of him.

Eureka just stared at Trace.

"Eureka…" The two had been getting along so well. Even when it was just her and the bird, he occasionally misbehaved, but Trace's presence made the mood swings more prevalent. "Off there," she repeated.

"He likes oranges, right? We can share one with him."

Traced cut an orange into sections, then showed a quarter

of a piece to Eureka before carrying it to the cage. Still watching Trace, Eureka stepped onto her hand.

This time, she didn't close the cage so that he didn't learn to associate treats with being closed in. As smart as he was, it wouldn't take him long to figure that out.

Trace added green peppers and onions to the omelets while she set the table. And fortunately, the coffee was ready, so she poured them each a cup.

After plating their breakfast, he joined her at the table.

"You frowned earlier." He'd waited until they'd had a few bites before speaking. "When I said I love pleasing subs."

"You surprised me." And he'd done so a second time by bringing it up, after all his warnings to avoid the conversation. She carved off a small section of her omelet but put down her fork without trying it. "That's not why I thought the Dom—Top—would be into BDSM."

"Tell me more."

She knew why she would be into it. The brain chemistry, subspace, made sense to her. Even thinking about it was enough to consume her. "I thought it was about the Dom issuing orders, getting the sub to do what he wanted so..." She took a breath when he sat back. Her words sounded ridiculous to her. "I'm messing this up, aren't I?"

"No. Not at all. I'm listening... I want to give you my full attention."

"Maybe I have some misconceptions, but I thought the Dom, the Top, got his joy from the power. From getting a woman to follow his orders."

"That would have a certain charm, I'll admit."

She could get lost in his eyes. A teasing smile curved his lips. Despite the tension inside her, he was teasing. "You're hinting that I haven't been the easiest client."

"In all honesty, querida? You've done much better than I

ever would. It's been three weeks. That's a long time to have your life turned upside down."

"You haven't been the worst jailer ever."

"Thank you. I think." Then, just as fast, his expression changed. "Back to your very serious question—maybe some Doms are in it for that reason, but I don't know anyone like that. Yes, I enjoy wielding the power that my play partner gives to me. I accept the honor and responsibility with the greatest respect. My true pleasure comes from watching her, drinking in her whimpers that fill the room, tracing the streaks of red on her skin. Her gratitude feeds my hunger."

He wove a spell so compelling that she wanted to step inside his world.

"If you didn't derive pleasure from it, neither would I."

She scooted back in her chair and curled her hands around her mug.

Eureka climbed out of his cage and made his way to the perch on top. He rang the bell and admired himself in the mirror, repeating, "Pretty bird."

"I want my sub to get off, to have exquisite orgasms."

His words rocketed through her, making her hot.

"I want her to be able to let go of her worries and stress, focusing only on herself."

"You make it sound like a spa day." She gave him a half-hearted smile, but he didn't return it.

"It's my responsibility to keep her safe so that she can get there."

Had he always been like that? Protective, with a hero complex? Compelled by duty to save the world?

"The more my partner trusts me, the deeper she can go, the more she can receive."

"Last night…"

He waited. Not that it surprised her. He knew what he wanted, and if patience was the way to secure it, he'd take all the time it required. It was comforting. And a bit confounding. "I wanted to know how you'd—we'd—proceed if..." She crossed her arms on top of the table. "You know."

"No. I don't know. And this is too important for me to make guesses."

"If I wanted to learn more."

"How much do you want to know? What do you want to know? It's one thing to talk about it, and knowledge is good, but there is no amount of talk or reading, even watching videos, that can adequately prepare you for the real-world experience of someone being solely focused on you, your pain inextricably bound to your pleasure. Theory is one thing. Experience, another."

A shiver rippled through her. "I meant..." She looked at him pleadingly. But he continued to regard her in silence, not making it any easier for her. "I'd like..." She blew out a breath. "Hypothetically, if you were interested, what would we do first?"

"Before we began, I'd want to learn about you, discover what intrigues you, what turns you on, what satisfies you. *Hypothetically,* I'd touch you, explore you, see where your pain threshold is. I might start with a few commands to see how you respond, if you're willing—or able—to give up control. It might be that you just like a little kink in the bedroom, a blindfold, a soft pair of cuffs. To be clear, whatever your preferences are, they're fine. There's nothing wrong with that."

She was pretty sure she wanted more than that.

"You have nipple clamps."

So he had found her toys that first day when he rummaged through her bedroom. After the conversation they'd been having, nothing should have embarrassed her, but it did.

"Do you play with them?"

She took a drink of her cooling coffee, stalling though she didn't know why. "I do."

"Has anyone ever put them on you?"

"No."

"But…? You've thought about it? Wanted it to happen?"

The confession was difficult. "It's sometimes part of my fantasies."

"Mine too. I love tormenting a woman's nipples, just at the edge of what she likes, not too much. The exact right amount."

Which was how much, for her? She swallowed.

In the office, her phone rang. She glanced at the clock. Her heart fell. Trace had held her so spellbound that she'd lost track of her very real responsibilities. "My conference call." To discuss ideas for correcting the code so that the mosquito injection mechanism achieved a ninety-nine percent effective rate.

"If you're interested, this evening, after dinner, let me know. We can go as slow as you want. Or not at all."

The phone rang again, yet she hesitated before dashing to answer.

Trace's eyes were rich, beckoning. Tempting. She wanted to trust him. She wasn't sure if she dared.

CHAPTER FIVE

HAWKEYE

A fter their dinner of a frozen pizza—and the nerves that had made it impossible to think—Aimee fled to the bathroom.

She turned the taps on and added a heap of salts. Lavender, she understood, was relaxing, not that it ever worked for her. After testing the temperature with her toes, she clipped her hair up, then stepped into the water. Steam rose, and she sank in to rest her head on the rim as water rose around her.

Ever since she and Trace had returned from their run this morning, Aimee had tried to act as if it were an ordinary day. It was anything but.

After her conference call, she'd lost herself in work before she stopped to take a shower. The break in her concentration hadn't been good. Over and over, her thoughts returned to Trace, and that led to fantasies about what might be later in the day, if she found the courage to move forward.

Midafternoon, she and Trace had gone to the grocery store and the coffee shop. He'd been cordial but nothing more. He didn't bring up the evening ahead or anything about BDSM. It was as if their kiss had never happened and their deep discussions hadn't occurred. Whatever happened next truly was up to her.

She leaned forward to turn off the taps.

There were a million intelligent reasons for her to go to her bed instead of returning to the living room. The sound of his voice reached her, and it was oddly comforting to know she was so protected. He moved through each room, checking and rechecking locks, looking for anything out of the ordinary. He left nothing to chance.

Once she was sure he was no longer in this part of the house—Eureka's squawk of "Agent!" was proof of that—she leaned forward to pull the drain plug.

She'd made her decision. Trace had been right. Theory was one thing. Experience was another—like moving from a classroom to the laboratory. She may never have another chance to have this kind of experience, and certainly not with a man like Trace.

Wrapping herself in a towel, Aimee bypassed her dresser in favor of walking to her closet.

How was she supposed to dress for an introduction to BDSM?

If he'd invited her to a club, she could have gone shopping to order something appropriate. And sexy shoes.

As it was, her selection was limited. She skimmed past her one sexy black dress—too forward—in favor of a long casual T-shirt. She skipped a bra but pulled on a thong and a pair of shorts. Since her hair was wild from the humidity in the bathroom, she pulled it into a ponytail.

Barefoot, fighting a sudden surge of nerves, she walked into the living room.

Trace looked up from the documentary he'd been watching. He clicked the remote's Off button. "I wondered... Hoped." He stood.

"Uhm..." She floundered. She'd never been this uncertain before. Now that they were so close together, this seemed premeditated, shifting her sense of the world. The few times she'd had sex for the first time, there was a rhythm to the encounter. Dinner, a movie, holding hands, a sweet kiss, an inevitability. "I don't know what to do."

"I'll guide you. You can trust in that. In me." He rounded the couch to take her shoulders.

"Aimee!"

She looked over at Eureka. "Night-night."

He closed one eye, but she swore he regarded Trace suspiciously out of the other. "Night-night," she repeated.

Eureka turned his back on them.

"That crazy loro is too damn smart."

"I keep thinking the same thing." Eureka's interruption had allowed her a moment to regroup, and while she was still off-balance, her hand had stopped trembling.

Trace stood in front of her, overwhelmingly large. His black T-shirt hugged his chest. She couldn't remember if his arms had always been that developed or whether he seemed bigger because of their proximity.

For a moment, she fixated on the size of his hands. They were enormous. To think of them curved around her breasts or landing on her bare bottom… She shifted from side to side.

"Have you thought of a safe word?"

"Krypton."

"*Preciosa*, I think you're going to be my kryptonite. Nothing else on the periodic table you'd rather choose?"

"I like krypton."

"Krypton it is." An approving smile slipped across his features, and her heart fluttered in response. "Use it at any time. This isn't about terrifying you."

She already was.

"But about helping you learn about yourself. Is it the fantasy you want? Or the reality?"

He pressed a thumb beneath her chin to tip it back while he gripped her left shoulder with his free hand. His strength was undeniable. Yet she had no doubt he would let her go if she struggled.

Trace captured her gaze. With the force of his own, he compelled her not to look away. His scent, his masculine presence, overwhelmed her.

"I want to know everything about you. Be honest with me and yourself."

Surely that was his most difficult request.

"Don't hide, querida."

"You know I'm nervous." Ever since Jack had used her words against her, she'd been careful to disguise her vulnerabilities.

"Nervous?" he pressed. "Or frightened?"

For a moment, she considered his question. "I'm not scared."

His smile sent her heart spiraling to her toes.

"Will you take out your ponytail?"

They both knew this was about more than her hair. He'd told her he'd give her commands to see if she would obey. In her books, the heroines were much braver than she was. They instantly complied, while she had a bucket of fear to contend with.

"It starts with a single step."

"What if it's the one that sends me off the edge of the cliff?"

"It will be," he promised.

His surety made her gulp.

Keeping her gaze fastened on him for strength, she pulled off the ponytail holder.

"Muss up your hair."

As if knowing what she needed, he continued to hold her. The last of her resistance melted. She fed her fingers into her hair, drawing some around her face, then toying with the strands until they teased her shoulders.

"Beautiful. But you're beautiful no matter what." He leaned in to capture her lower lip between his teeth, gently at first, then with a bit more force.

Rather than pulling away, Aimee surrendered. As she gave herself over to the slight pain, she found intense pleasure. *Yes.* This was what she'd craved. It was as exquisite as she dreamed.

He continued the pressure on her lower lip. Rational thought became impossible.

Subtly he changed what he was doing, demanding entrance to her mouth.

Willingly she surrendered.

She liked to be kissed, and this man knew how to kiss. He tasted of temptation and determination. There was no hiding from him or his demands.

Her arms went around him. She flattened one palm on his back, and with the other hand, she dug her fingers into his black hair. She raised on tiptoes to meet him more completely.

He was kissing her, and she was kissing him back.

Though they'd done this before, there was nothing similar about the experiences. Trace was more demanding as their tongues met in thrust and parry. She had a taste of what sex with him might be like, and she wanted more. His insistence awakened her, and the way he drew her tight and held her there gave her security she didn't realize she'd been lacking.

Slowly, he drew back, ending the kiss. "Your responses are exquisite."

The approval in his husky voice sent a tiny jolt of excitement through her. She'd taken that first step. Instead of terrifying, it was liberating.

"Shall we continue?"

Slowly, her lower lip throbbing, she nodded. Trace took his time releasing her before he took a couple of steps back.

"What are you wearing beneath the T-shirt?"

"Nothing."

"Show me."

His quiet command was a raw thrill, disconcerting and so different. Drawing a breath, she pulled the garment up, then off, dropping it to the floor.

"Oh, querida…"

That raw huskiness in his voice thrilled her. She'd never been with a man so appreciative.

"How do you play with them?"

"I…"

"Fight through your embarrassment." His voice was the encouragement she needed.

Aimee tipped back her head, closed her eyes, then used her forefingers to circle her nipples until they hardened.

"Beautiful."

She opened her eyes to see him staring at her. She needed him. "Will you touch me?" The words were more a plea than she'd intended. "I need your touch. I want to feel your hands on me. I want your mouth on my breasts, your tongue on my nipples." She lifted her breasts in invitation. "Please, Trace."

"It would be my pleasure." He was there for her, his arms around her, supporting her, one palm pressed against the small of her back, the other cradling her nape.

He lowered his head to capture a nipple between his tongue and top teeth. "I want to know what you like. Too much?"

"No. It's…" *Not enough.*

Then he sucked, hard, and her knees buckled.

He caught her, sweeping her from the ground and carrying her down the hallway to her bedroom.

"Please," she whispered.

"I haven't even started with you yet," he promised, setting her on the floor.

He put his pistol on the nightstand. She was so caught up with what he was doing that she didn't even protest the gun being in her bedroom. Her arms fell to her sides as she surrendered to him. He sucked her right nipple while he pinched the other between his thumb and forefinger. She arched her back, asking for more.

"Keep still," he ordered.

"Keep still?" Had he lost his mind? Because she was definitely losing hers. She'd never experienced anything like this, exquisite and painful, creating a demand from the inside out.

"Part of your lessons," he said, returning to her nipple and torturing it relentlessly.

She'd taken the first steps, she realized, and he was exerting his will more powerfully. He'd force her to be an active participant. Already she was learning there was nothing passive about being involved with him.

She began to squirm as heat flooded her body. She wanted more. More pressure. More intensity. She wanted to orgasm.

"Distract yourself," he said. "Think about something else, anything else other than how your body is responding to what I'm doing. Think about the fact I want you to keep still. Think about pleasing me."

"I…"

"Can," he told her. "You can. You're a runner. Breathe. Use the same techniques you use there."

"But—"

"Breathe." He sucked, gently at first, then with unyielding force.

She squirmed. She was coming undone. He couldn't possibly have any idea what he was asking of her, demanding of her. He'd assigned her a task, and she was doomed to failure. Staying still was nearly impossible with the way he tormented her. She'd never realized how sensitive her nipples were, never knew she could get so turned on from breast play.

She tried to follow his instructions.

When the only thing she could think of was how much she wanted to come, she forced her thoughts to her project and looming deadline. She met his gaze, saw the slight smile that toyed with his lips before he moved that skillful mouth to the tip of her other breast.

She wanted to do what he said, she realized, wanted to please him, wanted to see him smile at her.

He moved one of his hands between her legs. Helplessly, shamelessly, she ground her crotch against him, wishing she'd taken off her shorts. Even though she was dressed, he unerringly found her swollen clit and pushed his thumb against the sensitized nub. When she could no longer breathe in a controlled way, she settled for panting. Hearing his instructions echoing in her mind, she struggled to fend off the orgasm. But no matter how hard she tried to keep still, she couldn't.

He moved to her other nipple and bit. She cried out as a million tingles zapped through her.

Unexpectedly, an orgasm caught her. In a powerful and undeniable wave, it crashed into her, over her. "Oh, Trace!" She moved faster and faster against him, riding the wave of the climax, her pussy clenching.

He kept his mouth on her, his hand between her legs as she ground it out, damn near achieving a second orgasm.

When he finally moved away, her shoulders slumped forward. She was shattered. Complete. Overwhelmed.

Uttering soft, reassuring words that she couldn't quite understand, Trace wrapped his strong arms around her, offering support as he feathered a kiss against the top of her head.

Seconds later, when her breathing had returned to normal and her brain regained its functionality, she realized she was lying on the bed and he was beside her. She placed her head on his chest and said, "That never happens quite so fast."

"You're as responsive as I hoped." He traced one of her eyebrows.

She'd always believed there was something wrong with her, and Jack had reinforced that. When she'd been at college, her roommates had talked about their experiences, and she didn't have much to share in return. It seemed her friends enjoyed sex a whole lot more than she did. But now she was wondering if she'd just been with the wrong men.

"How are you feeling?"

"Satisfied." She wanted to wrap her arms around herself.

"Good. We're just getting started. I want you naked."

She eased back away from him a bit in order to meet his gaze. She saw tenderness in the depths of his brown eyes, but his jaw was set, the lines telepathing implacable power. She had waded into dangerous territory. Now there was nowhere to run. Nowhere to hide.

Even as she questioned whether or not she'd actually go through with it, she climbed off the bed and took a couple of steps backward.

Her nipples were still hardened into little pebbles, the cool whisper of air from the overhead fan keeping them taut.

She hooked her fingers beneath the band of her shorts and wiggled until they slid down her legs. She stepped from them, leaving them in a pile on the floor. They both knew she could have simultaneously removed her underwear, but she didn't have the guts for that.

"A thong?"

She nodded.

"Leaves your ass bare. Were you hoping for a spanking, Aimee?"

"No!"

He laughed.

"Well, maybe." He was right, but she didn't want to admit it to him, or even herself.

"It's pretty. But it needs to come off." He patiently waited while she discarded the scrap of material. The crotch was damp from her earlier climax and from the continual wetness his words caused.

Finally she stood there in front of him, bare. She tipped back her head, then folded and unfolded her arms a couple of times, not quite sure what to do with them.

"Lovely," he said. "I had no idea whether or not I'd find you shaven. I like it." His tone was rich with approval. "I would have shaved you myself."

The idea of having him so close, so intimate, while she was spread before him, vulnerable, sent goose bumps down her arms.

"When in doubt, keep your hands behind your back."

"Do you miss anything?"

"When it comes to you? Not ever, Aimee."

Having his attention so focused on her made her heady.

She moved her hands behind her back, and the act thrust out her breasts a little more.

"So pretty. I want your legs apart, regardless of whether you're kneeling or standing."

Kneeling? She gulped. Then, realizing he was waiting for her compliance, she spread her legs.

"Farther," he encourage. "Shoulder width, at least. I always want access to your pussy."

Her insides turned molten.

"That's it."

His constant approval made her want to please him more. He was a master of her seduction.

"Now face away from me."

She was reluctant to do as he said. Looking at him helped keep her grounded.

"Do as I say." His gruff tone let her know he wouldn't be disobeyed.

"Yes, Sir," she whispered. With trepidation, she followed his order.

"Now bend over and grab your ankles."

If she did so, with her feet so far apart, she would be totally exposed. Humiliation threatened to pull her into an undertow. She almost protested, but she stopped herself. He knew exactly what he was asking her to do and how much it would cost her emotionally to yield to him.

Trace didn't repeat his command. Instead, he waited, not touching her. Since he was behind her, she couldn't drink encouragement from his expressions. She was at a turning point. She could refuse, end this, maybe have hot sex, or she could go for it, embracing the things she'd always fantasized about.

Decision made, she hurriedly bent and grabbed her ankles—needing to do it before she changed her mind. The sight of the world upside down was too much, and she closed her eyes.

As she waited, schooling herself to be patient, she concentrated on the sound of the overhead fan and felt the air on her exposed parts, and she wondered what he was doing.

Looking at her, that was for sure. Thinking? Planning?

Enjoying the sight? Please God, she hoped he liked what he saw.

All her senses hummed, supercharged.

She inhaled the scent of him, that intoxicating blend of man and spice. She hungered for the sound of his voice.

"Almost perfect." He moved in behind her. He used his foot to exert pressure against the inside of her right ankle, forcing her into the position he wanted. "You're gorgeous. Everything about you."

He stroked her between the legs, long, sweeping motions with his large fingers. "Beautifully wet, Aimee." He parted her labia and glided a fingertip across her clit. "Your body is so honest."

Involuntarily she jerked.

"Try to keep still. Accept what I give you while I take what I want."

He feathered her clit again, and she gasped. But instead of moving, she squeezed her eyes shut even tighter and drew a deep breath.

"Quick learner," he said. He pressed a finger firmly on her clit. She moved forward a scant inch, trying to get away from the maddening, delicious intensity of the feeling. "Accept it," he reminded her.

He put a palm against the middle of her back, keeping her bent and preventing her from moving away. Then he increased the pressure on her tiny, already swollen nub.

"Trace," she murmured. Unbelievably another orgasm was already building inside. She told herself she could come from just this tiny amount of sensation, but she knew she was wrong. It wasn't just about his touch. It was about his mastery of her. It was the combination of the words he used and the force he exerted.

Even she could smell her arousal.

He began to move his finger in a tiny circle, and at the same time, with his palm, he pressed harder. "Focus."

She whimpered. Her hips began to sway, even though she fought against it. "Actinium," she said. "Aluminum. Americium."

"The periodic table?"

She didn't answer him. Instead, she focused. "Antimony…" She trailed off as he continued his relentless assault on her body. "Argon… Please! Please stop. Otherwise I'm going to come."

"Not yet."

"Trace!"

"Do as I say," he snapped.

Unbelievably, his sharp tone turned her on even more.

"I—"

"Breathe!"

Her knees threatened to give out. She could barely keep hold of her ankles. Thinking about anything except what he was doing was impossible. She needed to let him know that, but she couldn't find the words. "I…"

"Your orgasms are mine to give or deny. Fight it out, Aimee."

She did. Her eyes still scrunched closed, struggling for breath, she whispered, "Arsenic, astatine, barium…"

"Now." He slid a finger inside her. "Come now."

The orgasm swamped her. She lost her footing, and Trace grabbed hold of her, supporting her as he turned her, then scooped her from the floor and carried her to the bed. He lay down with her, careful to keep his boots off the mattress. He held her close, cradled her tenderly, her head on the soft material of his T-shirt.

"Thank you," she whispered. Until now she'd never understood why the female subs in the stories she read would be so appreciative after a climax. She figured they were because that was what their Doms demanded. Now she knew differently.

Her gratitude wasn't just for the earthmoving climax. It wasn't just because he'd relented and given his permission to come. Her gratitude was for all that and the way he read her so perfectly, recognizing what she needed, when she needed it, and for having her hang on longer than she might have so that the experience was even more meaningful. Most of all, it was for catching her, caring for her when she wasn't sure she was able to.

"That's a start, Aimee. Your introduction to turning over control."

She bunched his shirt in her fist, and he stroked his fingers down her spine, soothingly, possessively.

"When you're ready for more, I'll give you that spanking."

Before she thought it through, she swallowed. "I want to do that now."

"Now?"

"Yes." Get it over with, so that she would know whether it was for her or not. So far, what they'd done had exceeded her wildest dreams. But taking it further?

"You're sure? You don't need to think about what just happened?"

"I'm more sure of this than anything else.

"In that case, I want you to come find me when you're ready. Be naked."

"But…"

"I'm giving you a couple of minutes to think it through. I also want to check in with the team, look at the cameras."

She placed her hand on his chest and pushed herself up a little to meet his gaze. "I'm not going to change my mind."

His slow smile made her proud of her decision. "Good."

He untangled their bodies—when had she gotten so

wrapped up in him?—and slowly circled one of her nipples before sliding from the bed.

After watching him go, she collapsed against the pillow, her heart thundering. He moved through the house as if he owned it, his footsteps sure. He talked on his phone, and his voice was steady, in sharp contrast to the firmness that had undercut it while he was playing with her.

Heaven save her.

They'd played.

As each second ticked by, Aimee wished he hadn't given her time to reconsider. As the sexual high faded, she started to question herself. Who in their right mind walked naked to the living room and trusted the big badass agent there to spank her?

A few minutes later, silence shrouded the house. He'd finished his rounds, and he was waiting for her decision.

Until this evening, she hadn't realized how much was expected of a submissive. He made it clear that she had to be a participant at every turn. She had to go to him, without clothes, shedding her inhibitions. For a woman with as little experience as she had, it was a huge challenge.

But to get what she wanted, she had to follow through. Forcing aside her hesitations, she left the bed to join him.

He was seated in the dining room, and when she drew close, he put his phone facedown on the table and looked at her. "This is a surprise. A very pleasant one."

Earlier, he'd given instructions, been there as she undressed, but standing before him like this was ten times more difficult than it had been earlier.

Remembering his requirements, she placed her hands behind her back and spread her legs.

"Very, very well done."

"I… Thank you? Am I supposed to say that?"

He grinned. "You can say whatever you like. Tell me why

you're here."

Really? He was going to make her say it? "Uhm, for a spanking."

"Nervous?"

"In college, I'd ask if I could take tests early."

"Masochistic tendencies. I like that." He stood, picked up his chair, then moved it into the living room before taking a seat. "Come here and lower yourself across my lap."

"Is it possible to take it easy? I mean, virgin spankee and all that."

"Ah." He laughed. "No."

"It was worth a try." Behind her back, she twisted her fingers together.

Each step toward him was like trudging through quicksand. This was nothing like her fantasies. There, she was fearless, welcoming everything her Dom threw at her.

The reality was so different.

Her heart raced, and her brain cells had scattered.

Trace extended his hand. She slid her palm against his, but he didn't squeeze it reassuringly. Aimee had never suspected that she'd turn to him for comfort, even though he intended to deliver pain. The realization bent her thoughts in a dozen directions.

"To be clear…"

Since he was sitting and she was standing, they were eye to eye. His gaze was all-seeing. "Yes?"

"You may not come."

She almost laughed. "You're forbidding me from orgasming from a *spanking?*"

He grinned, and for a moment, she almost forgot to be nervous. "If you do come, we'll have to start the spanking over."

No chance.

"Ready?"

She nodded.

He exerted a small amount of force on her wrist to bring her toward him.

He tipped her over, and her stomach landed on his powerful thighs. She was terribly aware of how much smaller she was than him. Of his strength and power.

She reached for the hardwood floor for stability, but couldn't quite touch it.

"Spread your legs."

A tendril of panic crawled through her, and the word *krypton* pinged around in her mind. Krypton, krypton, krypton. If her brain could have completed a circuit and gotten the word from her subconscious and out of her mouth, she might have used it.

As it was, in this position, even gravity worked against her, and her hair fell forward, framing her face, a few strands getting in her eyes. She used her abdominal muscles to lift herself, but he pressed her back down.

This was terrifying. Exhilarating.

"You okay?"

She thought she nodded, but he prompted, "Aimee? I need you to answer me."

Was she okay? She was terrified. Excited. Anxious. "Yes," she managed.

He rubbed her rear, and she liked the feel of his hand on her. When he dipped a couple of fingers between her legs, she was stunned to feel dampness there.

"You were made for this, Aimee."

She forgot to be self-conscious. If he'd just touch her *there...*

"Now point your feet inward."

She fought against her natural inclination to refuse, to protect herself as much as possible.

"Point your feet inward," he repeated with as much

patience as he'd made the original command. "Good girl," he said when she did as instructed.

She hadn't been aware of following his order, but there was something hypnotic about him that compelled her response.

He rubbed her skin, making her relax, with what she guessed was a false sense of security. He moved on to more vigorous strokes, increasing her anxiety a couple of notches.

"How many for your first experience?"

She wanted to be brave. "Eight."

"Not nearly enough. Ten."

Why had he even asked?

"Count them for me."

Before she was fully prepared, the first one landed hard on her buttocks. She yelped. Good God, *it hurt*. She started to squirm. Some people actually liked this? Were they out of their minds? This was not what she'd expected.

But then he was there, soothing the hurt with his palm.

"Count," he reminded her.

"One," she whispered. Then, a second spank landed. "Damn!"

"Damn is not a number," he said, and she was sure she heard amusement in his voice, which meant at least one of them was enjoying this. "I can repeat it, if you wish."

"No! It was two." She wiggled. He placed a hand on the small of her back, effectively imprisoning her.

He spanked her again.

"Three!"

He rubbed over the sore spots, and she was surprised how soothing that was.

The moment she exhaled, he delivered another swat.

She moaned, but didn't cry. "Four."

"Much better. Relax into it."

"Relax into it?"

"If you fight it, your muscles will be tense. And you'll enjoy it less."

"Enjoy it. Right." Since she was still imprisoned, hanging upside down, she couldn't draw a full breath, and her words were muffled.

"I hope you do," he said. "I want you to."

He stroked between her legs, unerringly finding her clit. She moaned and shifted, trying to encourage him to put more pressure there.

"Naughty girl," he said.

He took away his hand, and she whimpered in protest.

He placed the next spank at that tender spot on her right side, on her thigh, right below her buttock.

She gasped but somehow managed the word "five."

He delivered the next one to her left thigh.

"Six." She whimpered. Tears swam in her eyes. She was barely over the halfway mark. Forty percent more to go.

"You're fighting." With extreme gentleness, he rubbed her tender areas. "Remember to breathe." He slid a hand between her legs again.

No way could this be arousing her.

"You look so beautiful," he told her.

His words did something to her, just like what happened when she read. She had never had a man's words so turn her on before. But the appreciative tone in his voice almost made it all worthwhile.

He spanked her three times in quick succession. The pain was so fast, so stinging, she couldn't even count.

"Seven, eight, and nine," he said.

Somehow, though, the pain receded quickly, leaving her warm. The overhead fan turned slowly, cooling the droplets of sweat that dotted her back.

Trace—her Dom—masturbated her. She was wetter than she ever remembered being. Her hips began to jerk, from the combination of his touch and the heat in her buttocks and thighs. Her toes dug into the floor as she struggled for control.

"I wish you could see what you look like," he said. "How desirable. Feel how hard my cock is from looking at your red ass."

"Trace!" Despite his earlier warning, the beginnings of an orgasm began to unfold. It didn't matter how much she told herself it was impossible. It was real. "Stop," she begged. "Please. Spank me. Spank me!"

"You'd rather I do that than stroke your swollen clit?"

"Yes!" The word was somewhere between a demand and a plea.

He drew some of her dampness over the nub. His finger slipped effortlessly, and she was going to go out of her mind.

"To be clear, you'd prefer me to stop doing this?"

Her body became rigid as she forced away thoughts of her impending orgasm. Silently she started through the elements of the periodic table again. *Actinium. Aluminum. Americium. Antimony. Argon...*

But it wasn't working.

The man was diabolical. Diabolical and good. He knew exactly what he was doing, just how to touch her to make her shatter. He could keep her on the edge as long as he wanted. But just as frightening, maybe more frightening, she knew he could force her past it at any moment.

Arsenic.

Now there was a good element

Arsenic, arsenic, *arsenic.*

"Please..." She wasn't thinking about *krypton.*

"You're not going to come, are you?"

He slid a finger inside her, and she bucked against him. He fucked her with it for long, torturous minutes before pulling it out again.

She was no longer certain what she was begging for. For him to keep it up until she climaxed, or for him to stop so she wouldn't have to start the punishment again.

"Tell me what you want."

"Spank…spank me!"

He still had one hand pressed against the small of her back. The other, he rested across the fleshiest part of her butt cheeks. Even though he wasn't touching her intimately, her pussy was throbbing. She was still ready for him.

"Ask me again, nicely, for the last one."

Something had changed inside her. She was turning herself, her reactions, over to him. A moment ago, she didn't think she could survive to the end.

Recalling what he'd told her, she focused on the last one, exhaling and spreading her legs again, without being told.

"You are a quick study, Miss Inamorata."

Nothing she did would change his pace, so she patiently waited on him.

"Last one. You will feel this, and you will remember it."

"Yes, Sir."

"Oh, Aimee…"

He spanked her exposed vulva.

She screamed, her body going rigid as the pain ripped at her.

Instantly she was in his arms, but instead of holding her as she expected, he carried her to the couch and placed her on the edge. He knelt on the floor and placed her legs over his shoulders.

No. He wouldn't. She couldn't… "Trace…"

With his strong hands, ones that had just relentlessly spanked her, delivering unimaginable pain, he kept her thighs spread wide apart. He kissed her tortured pussy, then licked her with long, slow strokes.

She tried to escape, but she was helpless.

He took away the pain and simultaneously made it worse. "I—"

"Come for me," he said. He entered her with two fingers, stretching her, seeking and finding her G-spot.

An orgasm, all the more intense from the physical assault on her private parts and mental assault on her thought process, swamped her.

She was dragged under, gasping and panting.

And when she recovered, he was holding her, trying to tame her messy hair. She blinked, unsure what to think, how to feel.

"How was your first spanking?"

It wasn't just the spanking, though. It was her first submissive experience, and it was the first time a man had ever gone down on her. Any of the three would have been enough, but to combine them into a single encounter altered her.

Aimee sought the right words to let him know what she was feeling. Nothing came to her. It was difficult to believe she'd won a spelling bee in elementary school, when right now she wasn't sure she could spell her own name—her first one, not her surname. She settled for "Unimaginable."

"Go on."

She should have known he wouldn't let her get away without elaborating. "A little confusing, maybe."

He waited without question.

"When you had me over your knee…"

"Were you tempted to use your safe word?"

"I was, at the beginning. For a few seconds, I thought I might panic when I realized how vulnerable I was. If my mouth would have worked—well, for anything other than gasping—I might have used it. But then you kept talking to me."

"I've never seen anything quite as spectacular as the sight

of you across my lap. When you turned your toes inward, spreading your cheeks, parting your labia to expose all of your pussy, believe me, spanking you was about the last thing on my mind. I've never been with anyone like you, Aimee, and I want you to know that."

She met his gaze. No other man had ever had this kind of talk with her. "You seemed to know that I needed your touch. Then I knew you were watching me, it was… Disconcerting at first. And now, with you demanding to know what I was thinking, for me to describe my experience…" She shrugged. "It's as if I can't hide or keep secrets from you."

"When BDSM is part of a relationship, honesty is even more important."

"I see that." She nodded. "I guess the unexpected thing is how liberating I found the whole thing."

"Liberating?"

"I was able to give myself over to the experience totally. I stopped being self-conscious. And I think it's a bit odd that I did get off from the pain."

"Erotic pain," he corrected. "Deliberately inflicted, placed, and timed. I watched you every step of the way. I saw the way you responded, and I played on that. If something hadn't been working for you, I would have changed it up. I doubt you'd get off from random pain."

"I'm puzzled, though, about… I was naked but you weren't."

"Deliberate as well. I wanted your introduction to be all about the act of your submission, not as a prelude to sex."

"I thought it was all connected." She frowned. "I mean… You don't want—"

"Are you asking if I want to be buried inside you, Aimee?"

She pulled her lower lip between her teeth. "I'm afraid of rejection. But yes. I want you, Trace."

CHAPTER SIX

HAWKEYE

T race needed her with a desperation that unsettled him, and the tremor of vulnerability in Aimee's voice nearly undid him. The combination was potentially lethal, and having sex with her would be emotionally risky. He might start thinking about a future with her, and the past had taught him the stupidity of that. "I would never reject you, my sweet Aimee."

They'd already crossed one line that they shouldn't have. He dared not cross the biggest. "You need to go to bed."

"But—"

"Aimee, we aren't going to conflate BDSM and sex." He meant that, and it was an excellent excuse, one that didn't involve him baring himself, admitting how much he desired her and how fucking enticing she was.

He slid her off his lap, ignoring the incessant throbbing in his dick. "I'm putting you to bed."

"I'm fine." She stiffened her spine.

Fuck. Hurting her emotionally hadn't been part of the plan. Trace scooped her up, despite her small kicks of protest. "I'm your bodyguard." He needed the reminder as much as she did.

"I can walk."

Striding down the hallway holding on to the wiggling, angry, beautiful woman was more difficult than he would have believed. "Keep still before I sling you over my shoulder." Where he could slap her ass for real. His sacrifice was for both of them.

In the bedroom, he placed her on the edge of the mattress, and she stood the moment he stepped back.

"That will be all, Agent Romero. Thank you."

He plowed his hand into his hair. "Aimee…"

"I've had enough of bossy, dictatorial men who think they know what's best for me and want me to conform to their wishes. I appreciate the reminder. Good night."

God*damn* it. "It doesn't need to be this way."

"Out." Naked, hair mussed, nipples erect, ass red, and seductively smelling of sex, she pointed at the door.

He sighed. If he'd made a different choice, she would be wrapped around him, the softness of her sighs filling the air.

Instead, he was banished. And she was hurt.

She thought he was a jerk, but that was better than the alternative.

He left the room, closing the door behind him with a *click.*

In the dining room, Eureka glared for a moment before turning his back.

Restless, Trace grabbed a flashlight from the countertop and headed into the backyard. The neighbor's dog growled softly, but it didn't bark like crazy. After completing a sweep, he went back inside, locked the door, then headed out the front to check in with the team.

Riley slid down the driver's window of the SUV parked up the block. "What's up, Romero?"

"Double-checking."

"Howdy," Bree Mallory said, putting down her energy drink. "We've been talking about it. We're willing to split the money with you."

Trace frowned. "What money?"

"If you help us figure out Ms. Inamorata's first name."

"Generous of you." Because he knew how grueling the hours of surveillance could be, he grinned.

"Well, we know for a fact it's not Donna, Ruth, Julie, or Louise, right? She seems more like a Prudence or Catherine or Christine. Something more formal, you know?" Mallory guessed.

"But her sister is Aimee. Informal," Riley countered. "So maybe it's a top-ten name, like Jennifer or Jessica. Maybe Emily."

"But look how Aimee is spelled—it's not traditional."

"Maybe it's like E-m-i-le-e."

"No one would do that." Riley looked at Trace. "I mean, right?"

How many times had the duo had the same argument? He started to move away, then turned and came back. "Don't let anything happen to her."

"No chance," Mallory promised, leaning over Riley. "I'm more frightened of Inamorata than I am of Hawkeye himself."

"See, you keep proving that Mensa IQ," Riley said.

"Night," Mallory called out.

Riley smothered a yawn.

"You're off at eleven, right?"

"Then for two long, glorious days. Laurents and Barstow will be filling in."

"Enjoy your weekend."

"I'm thinking of taking in a Rockies game, with too damn many beers."

"After sitting on your rear for five days?" Mallory scoffed.

"Well, what're you doing?"

"Getting my nails done. Being pampered."

They bickered more than any married couple. Trace rapped his knuckles on the roof, then left the two of them alone. After lifting a hand to the other team, Trace went back inside the house. Eureka looked at him without squawking, and everything was silent from Aimee's bedroom.

Tonight, for the first time, Trace would have traded his overnight with someone else. Staying on the couch while Aimee was snuggled up in her bed counted as cruel and unusual punishment.

———

PROVIDING PROTECTIVE DETAIL HAD NEVER BEEN HARDER.

Through the years, Trace had been assigned to plenty of challenging clients, and in some damn miserable places.

But nothing had exacted this kind of emotional toll.

The easy camaraderie he and Aimee had developed had vanished, buried beneath an avalanche of tension.

Ever since he sent her to bed alone three days prior, ice had frosted every word she uttered. He still made her meals, and she ate them in her office instead of at the dining room table. They ran, and she showed no mercy when setting the pace. Each evening, she'd worked late, then took her pad into her bedroom without saying good night.

He should count that as a blessing. Keeping his hands off her curvy, delectable body was difficult enough without adding temptation to the mix.

But he'd about had enough of the hostilities.

Trouble was, he didn't know how to end them.

Well, yeah, he did. But not without turning her over his knee and paddling her perfectly curved ass. Or kissing her senseless. Or finally fucking her until he'd exorcised the demon driving him to claim her. Maybe then he would find peace.

He'd taken her for a latte this morning, and then later they'd gone for a run. She didn't vary her schedule, even on the weekends. After showering, she'd told him she had a video conference scheduled for early afternoon, then she'd wheeled Eureka's cage into the office and shut the door.

Not that he couldn't—and wouldn't—go in. He checked the camera system periodically, at least once an hour.

He was on his second cup of coffee from a fresh pot when her excited "Yes!" reached him.

Instantly, Eureka ripped out a series of squawks.

After days of quiet, her enthusiasm was a welcome change. Curious, Trace poured her a cup of coffee—his version of an olive branch—and carried it down the hall.

Aimee was standing, leaning toward the computer monitor.

She didn't even glance over at him.

"Agent!"

"Hey, menace."

A number of people were on the screen, in a room he recognized as being at Hawkeye headquarters on the outskirts of Denver. There were a number of men and women high-fiving each other. Aimee's teammates? Some of the finest geeks outside of Silicon Valley? A woman wore a dress so rumpled it looked as if she might have slept in it. A couple of the guys had on geeky Star Wars T-shirts.

"Let's see how it works," one of the men said. He was in bright yellow, had hair halfway down his back, and appeared to be in his early twenties—if that old. Shockingly, he was in bare feet. At headquarters.

"You got it, Knoll."

Aimee gripped the edge of her workstation and leaned even farther forward.

Trace put down the cup and moved in closer to her.

Eyes wide, she worried her lower lip.

The camera focused on a woman behind a computer screen. Everyone in the room at Hawkeye fell silent. The woman moved her fingers quickly over the keyboard, and her screen changed from a string of code to an image of the room from the far corner.

Aimee exhaled and wrapped her hands around her chest. "Yes, yes, yes." This time, instead of a yell, her words were whispered.

The funereal silence at headquarters lifted, and yells ripped through the room. Eureka joined in as people celebrated with hugs and cheers.

"It worked…" She looked at him and blinked. "It worked."

"Congratulations."

"It's been years…" She turned to him. Her grin could light a small city, and energy vibrated off her.

Then because he couldn't help himself, he closed her in his arms. He had no idea what her triumph was, and it didn't matter. He was fucking elated that he was here for her.

"I can't believe this."

In the Hawkeye room, someone popped a bottle of champagne.

"There's still a lot of work to be done, but we're getting closer. We know it can be done—it just needs to be reliable."

After the days of unease and silence, having Aimee happy shattered something in him.

"You'll want to shut off your video if you're live."

"I was watching, not participating."

"Good." He kissed her, something quick, nonthreatening, inviting. How she responded was up to her. He'd demand nothing. She could move away, acting as if she'd been swept up in the moment.

Her eyes wide, she swayed into him, linking her arms around his neck. "Yes."

This time, his kiss was deeper, asking forgiveness for not accepting what she'd offered days before, atoning for the hurt he'd caused in trying to be a hero.

She accepted his unspoken apology with heat that made his cock hard.

When she pulled back, her mouth swollen, her eyes wide, she said, "I know what I want." She lowered her arms to her sides and took a step back. "And I don't need you saving me from myself."

"Aimee—"

"Don't." She placed a finger over his mouth. "Just don't, Trace. Give me that much respect. Listen to me. Stop trying to protect me from you. The only thing I need is your honesty. If you want me, then take me. If you don't, that's fine. Tell me."

He captured her wrist, his senses flaring. "Can you doubt it?"

"No." She exhaled. "Yes. You're so damn confusing. Fuck me, or make love to me, have sex. Whatever. Spank me. Teach me."

She was so earnest, he couldn't hold out any longer, even though his nobler nature urged him to do that. "I could have you up against a wall," he murmured into her ear. "With your arms over your head, keeping you helpless."

Her mouth parted slightly.

"Or bent over, with you grabbing your ankles so that I can admire your cunt while I put a finger in your ass."

Had the pretty professor known what she was asking for, demanding, when she kept asking him to fuck her? "Maybe on your back, spread-eagle, tied to the bed while I flog your pussy until your clit is swollen?" With reserved restraint, he sank his teeth into that tender spot where her neck and shoulder merged.

Her knees wobbled. "Or maybe something gentle, with you beneath me so I can see your expression when you come?"

His beautiful Aimee gasped. He'd never been much for tenderness, but she brought it out in him. "But this is about you being adventurous, isn't it?" His words painted colorful scenarios in his mind. He was so fucking hungry for her—crazy from the days of denying her—that he yearned to take her in every way possible. "In that case, perhaps, I should order you onto your stomach, spread-eagle, with a pillow underneath you, so your ass is begging for the spanking I'll give it."

"Oh, Trace…" Her words were so faint that he could hardly make them out.

"Are your nipples hard?" He bit her again, then laved away the hurt with his tongue. "Are they, querida?"

"Yes," she whispered.

"And your pussy. Is it wet for me?"

She blushed. Despite her bold words, she was still the innocent. That knowledge made him want her even more.

"Very."

"Which will it be? Tied to the bed? Up against a wall? Or bent over? And if the decision is being tied to the bed, faceup or facedown?" He released her wrist to grab her shirt and pull it up over her head. He tossed the material on the floor, and Eureka squawked. "Is he going to be okay?"

"Maybe I should put him in the cage."

It took her a couple of minutes to coax him into doing what she wanted, and he protested when she closed the door. "He seems protective of you."

"Uhm… The vet says they can be hormonal. Territorial. Some people recommend I get him a mate."

Two of them? Trace couldn't begin to imagine.

"Until now, it hasn't been a concern."

Until now, he hadn't been intent on making her his. He took her hand and led her to the bedroom. "Where were we?" He swept his gaze over her. Goose bumps dotted her arms, and her breaths were shallow. Her earlier words had been brave, but what was going on inside her told a different story. She was nervous as hell. And she was right to be.

After this, for him—for them—there would be no going back. "Undress for me."

Not even blinking, she slipped out of her sandals, making her several inches shorter. Then, looking at him, she wiggled out of her shorts, leaving her in a sheer black lacy bra and a pair of sexy briefs. "Panties next."

"Yes, Trace."

Her words were a gift.

She stripped them off, then stepped out of them.

"How are you supposed to stand?"

Aimee worried her upper lip as she spread her legs.

Trace pressed his palms together so as to avoid the temptation of touching her. Not quite yet. Because when he did, he would lose all restraint. "Now remove your bra."

Once she had, she remembered to place her hands behind her back, thrusting her breasts toward him.

Her hair was in a ponytail, so she couldn't hide behind the strands, allowing him to see her expressions—trepidation, excitement, and the most intoxicating of all, trust. "Now, undress me."

"I'm not quite sure where to start."

"Go with your intuition."

The air scented with her sweetness, she took two steps toward him. He remained in place, wanting to own every second of her innocent seduction.

Her motions hesitant, she tugged his shirt free from his

waistband. Then she pulled up, her pinkie fingers brushing his abs. He sucked in an involuntary breath, and she smiled.

Once his shirt was off, she hung it from a bedpost.

He sat on the mattress. "Boots."

With a tiny nod, she knelt before him. Remembering his prior instructions, she spread her legs apart. "So damn lovely."

She tugged off each of his boots and socks, then looked up.

Trace stood, extracted his wallet from his back pocket, then pulled out a condom. He tossed both onto the nightstand before prompting, "Now the rest."

Her fingers a little unsteady, she unbuckled his belt, then unfastened the button on his waistband before lowering his zipper.

Then she tugged down his jeans.

Since he was commando, his erect cock sprang free, inches from her lips, close enough that her warm breath washed over him.

"Oh my." She remained where she was, looking up at him. "God."

"I take it you approve?"

"I… Yes."

He grinned as he offered her a hand up. Because he wanted to be inside her, he lifted her onto the bed and pushed her back. He knelt between her legs and licked between her delicate folds.

"Trace, I'm so ready for you."

"Are you, querida?" He dipped a finger inside, sliding back and forth, making certain she was fully lubricated.

Whimpering, she gripped his shoulders. He circled her clit, and she lifted her hips in silent entreaty.

He plunged his tongue inside her, and she ground her pelvis against him. Such a hot, beautiful woman. He was proud of her as she tossed her head back and forth and fisted the bedsheets, staving off an orgasm.

When he was certain she was on the verge of shattering, her whimpers becoming gasps, he moved away.

"Trace…"

He left her just long enough to roll on the condom. "I want your legs over my shoulders."

With a nod, she raised her legs, and he pressed against the backs of her thighs, keeping her wide for his entrance.

"That's so… Wow."

"Relax." He pressed forward, sliding in a fraction of an inch at a time. Despite her arousal, she was so damn tight.

He eased out to lick her again and glide a thumb across her mouth.

"It's been a while." A blush highlighted her cheekbones.

"You're perfect." He claimed her mouth, and when she closed her eyes to give herself over, he slid his cockhead inside her again.

He continued to kiss her, deeply, in silent reassurance.

A few seconds later, tension left her body, and she began to move with him, offering more of her body to him.

When he sank in all the way, he groaned, the sound buried between their mouths. Yeah, he was making love to her. And it was unlike anything he'd ever done. He wanted to satisfy her, let her know he cared, that she wasn't just an assignment.

Trace ended the kiss, then changed his position a little so he could tease her pussy. Her lips parted, and she tipped back her head. Ordinarily, missionary wasn't his preferred position, but with her, it might be his favorite. Her face was so expressive, he wanted to savor each reaction.

She gripped his shoulders. "I'm…" She dug her fingernails into his skin, nearly sending him over the edge as the climax rippled through her.

Her internal muscles squeezed his cock, and he gritted his back teeth to hold off as long as he could.

But he hadn't counted on his reaction to her.

Her pleasure drove his, and he surged forward, his shoulders forcing her legs even wider as he ejaculated.

He took care not to collapse on her, and instead pulled out, then rolled to his side and pulled her against him.

She curled into him. He ran his fingers up and down her arm as he waited for his breathing to return to normal. Not that there ever would be a normal for him again.

Aimee placed a hand on his chest, like a longtime and familiar lover would do.

"You okay?"

"I might be sore," she said, her voice slightly teasing. "But if so, it's worth it."

"You deserve some time to recover," he said. "You've earned it. Before I fuck you again."

Using her hand as leverage, she pushed herself up to meet his gaze. "Do you mean that?"

"Querida. I mean it. I'm going to make sure you're completely satisfied. And I want to take you from behind."

CHAPTER SEVEN

HAWKEYE

"**A**gent!"

At Eureka's greeting, Aimee turned from her workstation to look over her shoulder at Trace. Not that she didn't know he was there. When he was near, the atmosphere sizzled.

Damn, he looked so appealing, especially now that she knew what he looked like beneath his T-shirt...and jeans. She swallowed in an attempt to hide her all too feminine reaction.

"Dinner's getting close. When you join me, I'll throw the steaks on."

"Thanks."

"Wine?"

"Maybe a small glass." To settle her nerves.

He nodded.

"Thank you." She blew out a breath as he walked back down the hallway, leaving his stamp on the air around him.

She wasn't sure how she'd she survived the afternoon.

Before they'd had sex, she'd told him, and herself, that she knew what she was doing. She couldn't have been more wrong.

The taste of BDSM that he'd given her earlier in the week had been everything she hoped it would be. And she'd surmised that sex would be fabulous, and that the orgasm would be stunning. It had been, but she hadn't expected that he'd be such a thoughtful lover.

When he realized she was struggling to take him fully, he'd eased out and made it easy for her. Then, when the orgasm had taken over, emotion had crested with it. She clung to him, and he'd held her while her breathing returned to normal. It had taken much longer than it should have. She rationalized that the situation was unique, that the fact that he was her bodyguard peppered her senses with a sense of danger. But as she rested against him, she'd realized that wasn't true. She was starting to care for him. And that was the reason the tension between them had been so unbearable.

Seeking some sense of normalcy, she tightened her pony-tail before standing and walking to Eureka. He was standing on the perch atop his cage. "I'm taking you for a ride." The moment she started to push, he protested, flapping his wings madly, before landing on her shoulder with a loud squawk in her ear. Another plan that hadn't gone as well as she'd hoped.

She immediately transferred him to her hand, then carried him into the dining room where she placed him on a perch.

The sight of Trace in her kitchen, in front of a cutting board, knife in hand, still sent little shivers through her. He'd already taken time to set the table and fill water glasses. He'd prepared a salad and mixed it in a glass bowl. "Anything I can do to help?"

"I've got it under control. Your wine is over there." He nodded to the counter next to him.

She skirted behind him and grabbed the goblet before leaning against a cabinet to watch him.

With the back of a large knife, he slid diced tomatoes into a bowl before slicing a jalapeno in half to scoop out the seeds. "Successful afternoon?"

She seized on the conversation, anything to pretend her tummy wasn't in turmoil. "It was. This morning's video gave a lot of us inspiration to work through the day."

"I'm curious, obviously."

Her sister had given Aimee permission to tell Trace as much as she deemed appropriate. After all, they were constantly together and sharing office space.

"We're working on a microchip that's so small, it can hardly be detected. We attach it to a bug. It could be something that resembles a mosquito or a butterfly, or even a bird." She took a small sip of the rich red wine. "The bug can be controlled remotely."

"Like the drones being used by the military?"

"Precisely. It's kind of obvious that we could use them to survey terrain."

"With a bird." He added the diced jalapeno to the tomatoes.

"Yeah. And no one is likely to kill a butterfly."

He nodded.

"We have programmers all over the world working on the project, and we each work on teams to develop specific technology. And of course, there are teams that work on integration of all the parts. It's much more complex than you might imagine."

"Which team are you on?"

"Deliverability."

He glanced over. "Meaning?"

"Our mosquitos can land on a person or animal and sting

them, for lack of a better term. In reality, we will be injecting them with a chip."

"Jesus."

"This morning's attempt was successful. As you saw on the monitor, we were able to track the subject's motions and actions. In the future we hope to listen in to conversations."

"This has all kinds of applications for the military."

She rolled the globe of the wineglass between her palms.

Trace turned to her. "Hawkeye is a government contractor on this?"

"I can neither confirm nor deny that."

"What if it falls into the wrong hands?"

A number of ethical conundrums had run through her mind, and she'd reached her own sort of peace. "Obviously there are a lot of concerns about the technology."

"Privacy."

Aimee nodded. "Among other things." She loved her work, but due to the sensitive nature of it, she rarely had the chance to talk about it. Her social circle was somewhat limited, and she spent most of her time communicating through email or on chat with other teammates. If she didn't go out for her daily latte, her voice would probably dry up from disuse. "Let's say we're hired to protect the daughter of a company president, but she doesn't want a detail. Should we be allowed to chip her without her knowledge? Or her pet, or what about her pillow? And if we're trying to infiltrate an organization—say we're trying to rescue a kidnapped businessman in Colombia—we need intel, and this is a way to get it. Most people would say that's a good use of the technology."

"Agreed."

"But what if a man suspects his wife is cheating on him? Should it be okay for him to chip her, or the Chihuahua she puts in her purse before she goes out? Do the ends justify the means?"

"When you work on something with the potential for good and evil in the same package, it has to keep you awake at night."

"You might think so. The potential benefits are enormous. And I also believe that others have to be working on similar things, right? Nanotechnology isn't new. You can bet bad guys have teams on it, and so do enemy governments. We must be ahead on this. How do we know this isn't already being used on our soldiers, our state department representatives, even elected officials?"

"Do you have the chip here?"

"Absolutely not." She shook her head. "I'm not a hardware person. So there's nothing here that would be of interest. The security around the project is immense. Even if someone found out about it, what would lead them to me? That's why I think the break-in was random. I'm not as concerned as..." She trailed off. "That's why I'm not as concerned as my sister seems to be," she said instead.

"You almost said her name."

"Did not." Not under penalty of death.

"Jennifer?"

She shook her head.

"Susan?"

She laughed.

"Mandy?"

"Mandy? No." Her sister's first and middle names were top secret at Hawkeye. Aimee had been sworn to secrecy, and it generally wasn't difficult to avoid mentioning them since she worked remotely.

"I'll get it out of you."

His eyes turned molten, and instantly she was back in the bedroom, her mind clouded with images of him. And no doubt he could get her to reveal almost anything. "Dinner," she reminded him. "Steaks."

"Right. Dinner."

She glanced down into the depths of the wine.

Trace went outside, and she forced herself away from the sudden memories long enough to segment an orange to add to the salad. Then she sprinkled pine nuts on top. She used tongs to move a small portion into a bowl for Eureka before tossing in feta cheese.

When he returned, Trace added more salt to the pico de gallo, then opened a bag of corn chips.

Aimee scooped up a taste test. "If this whole security operative thing doesn't work out for you, I'm willing to consider hiring you as a chef."

"Thank you. I think."

Within a few minutes, he'd plated the steaks, and they were seated across from each other.

"This dinner really is amazing," she said after her first bite.

"Passes the time when I'm on a detail. And nothing beats a good meal. I enjoy the cooking. Now if I can get Mom to turn over control of the Thanksgiving turkey to me…"

Once she finished her glass of wine, she stood to grab the bottle from the counter.

"I'd prefer you didn't."

"Oh?"

"I promised I wasn't done with you. Safe, sane, consensual," he reminded her.

Unsteadily, she put the bottle back down and swallowed deeply. She rejoined him at the table, and the excited nerves chasing through her took away her appetite.

Though they chatted about his family and their holiday celebrations, she couldn't stop thinking about what was going to happen later. And she'd never been happier a meal ended.

"I'll load the dishwasher while you prepare yourself for me," Trace said.

"Prepare myself?"

"I'll meet you in the bedroom, where I expect to find you naked and kneeling with your nipple clamps draped over your open palms."

Her heart skidded to a stop.

"Any questions?"

She tried to make her mouth move, but it didn't.

He lifted an eyebrow. "Querida?"

"I'm…"

"You could try 'Yes, Trace.' Or 'Yes, Sir.'"

Her mind went into freefall. "Yes,…Trace."

She turned to flee. When she reached the bedroom door, he called her name. Instantly she froze and looked in his direction.

"On second thought, get out all of your toys and place them on the nightstand, along with the lube."

To steady herself, she grabbed the doorframe.

"Don't dawdle."

Her world tilted. Her introduction to BDSM had been stunning in its physicality and her emotional response to it. She'd expected sex with him to be like fucking, hot but disconnected. Instead, his tenderness had seeped through her defenses. This time, he was going a different direction. Not knowing what to expect was scary and delicious.

She tugged open the drawer with her personal items and removed the lube. Shaking, she lined up the butt plug next to it. That, she hoped, he didn't intend to use. She'd bought it because it was on sale and because she was curious. But she'd never quite had the guts to try it. Her one attempt at anal sex in college had ended in disaster, enough so that she had never attempted it again.

In the kitchen, the faucet turned off, which meant she was running out of time. And of course, ever vigilant, he checked in with the team for an update.

She pulled out her vibrator and the nipple clamps before kicking off her shoes and taking off her clothes.

Quickly, she knelt, the chain from the clamps draped over her extended palms. At the sound of his boots on the hardwood floor, she remembered to spread her thighs farther apart.

"Beautiful." He entered the room to stand directly in front of her.

How had she not realized what this would be like, with him so large and dominating, filling her vision? No wonder kneeling was so common in the books she read. There was something significant to being in a helpless position, waiting for instructions.

He crouched in front of her and placed his knuckles beneath her chin. Then, he slid two fingers between her legs, glancing a touch across her clit.

She moaned, leaning into him.

"Stay where you are, please."

How could she?

He entered her with the same two fingers, then spread them apart. Needing to hold on to him, she lost her grip on the clamps, sending them clattering to the hardwood floor.

"That was unfortunate." He gently pinched her clit, and she pitched forward. "Shall I pick them up for you, querida?"

"Uhm, yes." God, she was overwhelmed. He was so damn sexy, the pinch had hurt, but pleasure chased it away. "Please."

"Extend your hands again, please." He scooped up the clamps and hung the chain from her hands. "This time, do what it takes to hold them in place." His words were soft but unrelenting as he slid between her folds again, gently abrading her clit with a thumbnail.

To shut out the overwhelming sensations, she closed her eyes. *Boron. Bromine. Cadmium.*

"That's perfect, Aimee. Now…" He pulled away his hand. He stood while she blinked the world back into focus. "Put the clamps on your nipples. Show me how you do it."

She fumbled with the chain but this time managed to hold on.

"Yes, Trace," he prompted.

"Yes, Trace."

"Those may be my favorite words." He folded his arms and watched her.

Calcium. Californium. Shoving aside her sense of mortification, Aimee played with her left nipple until it was swollen. Then, being careful, she went to set the clamp in place. She fumbled slightly, and the pinchers caught just the tip. She yelped and pulled away the vicious little teeth.

"Would you like a little help?"

Breathless, she looked up at him. "If… Yes, Trace."

He brushed her fingers aside and took hold of her nipple. At first he was gentle, soothing away the hurt, but as sexual response flowed through her, he squeezed a little harder, then tugged it out, elongating the flesh. "Now put it on."

This time, she managed to affix the thing correctly, not that it was much better. "Will you help with the other one as well?"

"If you have difficulty."

She had a sense that he enjoyed that, even if it was just a little.

It took her two attempts to set the second in place.

"They look very pretty."

His tone made the ache bearable.

"I want you on the bed, querida. Sit on the edge."

As she stood, the chain swayed, and the little teeth seemed to bite deeper. Pleasure swept straight to her pussy, making her moan.

"You knew."

She frowned at him.

"How good it would be. BDSM. Involving your mind, your body, your imagination."

"Honestly?" She sought the right words. "Better. Reading about someone else's experiences is one thing, but, I guess… The way you pinched my clit? So unexpected. It hurt, yet it was so appropriate, and so wonderful. Nothing could describe it."

He nodded.

She moved slowly, minimizing her motions as she perched on the edge of the bed.

"Tell me about your butt plug."

"I bought it on a whim, but I've never used it."

"Until me."

She didn't answer. Couldn't.

He pulled out a condom and dropped it on the nightstand before undressing. His beautiful cock was already hard and pointing in her direction.

Surprising her, he picked up the tiny vibrator, then tested it on his finger, sliding the speed bar up and down and tested each setting, from a flutter, to an intermittent pulse, to a constant thrum. "Is it powerful enough for you?"

"Yes."

He flicked it off, then squeezed a dollop of lube onto the little nubs before offering it to her. "Lay back and raise your legs."

Fearing what was next, she did as he said. The chain swayed, pulling on her nipples. Then Trace took her hips and pulled her forward, until only part of her buttocks remained on the mattress. If she tried to lower her legs, her shifting weight would pull her out of bed.

"Turn the vibrator on pulse and hold it against your clit. Keep it there."

She did as he said while he rolled the condom on. Trace stood there, stroking his shaft as she pressed the wiggling device against her pussy.

"Keep your legs apart so I can see. You wouldn't want me to have to devise a spreader bar."

"Of course not, Trace." Though she'd never admit it, the threat thrilled her.

Watching him stroke off was ultrahot, shoving her toward an orgasm. Then the device let out a strong pulse. She jerked her hips, almost toppling from the bed. Her abs struggled to hold her in place. The man was diabolical.

"How wet are you?" Obviously his question was rhetorical since he slid a finger inside her to check for himself.

Her pussy clenched in response.

He eased out his finger and placed his cockhead at her entrance. He gripped the chain running between her nipples and gave an exquisite tug, making her arch toward him. "Are you ready for me, Aimee?"

"Yes, yes!"

The angle and her complete submission gave him incredible access. He stroked in and out, deeper each time as her body responded to him.

Then his shoulders were against her legs, giving him greater leverage, placing her even more at his mercy.

She was splintering.

"Take me, Aimee. All of me."

Finally, she was filled with him, and he leaned into her. She cried out. He was so big. Relentless. And the pain shooting through her nipples, the persistent pulse on her clit.

Carbon. Cerium. Cesium.

"Hang on for a moment." He eased out, then gyrated his hips, his cock angling against her G-spot.

"Trace!"

"Move the vibrator away."

Grateful, she dropped her hand to her side.

"Leave it on, and keep hold of it."

It pulsed in her palm, and she would swear her pussy clenched as if it were still in place. She shuddered as the ripples built in her.

He moved the chain so that it was near her face. "Open your mouth."

She widened her eyes. He couldn't be serious.

"I mean it, Aimee. Do as I say."

In order to obey, she had to lift her head a little, which meant if she tried to lie down, she'd put unbearable pressure on her nipples.

Still, wild with desire, she opened her mouth.

"Don't let it go."

She started to nod, but the tugging sensation brought her back to the edge of a climax. *Cesium... Cesium.* Suddenly she had no idea what came next.

"Now give me the vibrator."

"But…"

He gave her pussy a hard little smack.

She screamed and immediately offered the vibrator.

"Excellent." When he pressed it against her, he didn't set it to a tiny, annoying pulse. Instead, he selected a rapid hum.

Unable to hold off, she cried out and climaxed. Her head dropped back, pulling off the clamps, making her scream and come a second time.

He moved the vibrator away and turned it off. "That was worth the wait, wasn't it?"

She gasped for breath and met his gaze. It had been.

Trace had given her the most intense orgasm of her life. A

wave of something she didn't dare name swept through her. But it left her vulnerable. She told herself it was natural, a result of a powerful reaction. Nothing more.

Somewhere deep, she recognized her own lie.

"I do like watching your reactions, querida." He pressed his thumb to her, and the pressure, without movement, was soothing. He resumed fucking her, this time in long strokes.

Surrendered, she relaxed, enjoying the less frenetic pace. She caught her breath as she moved with him.

"You fit me well." He leaned farther forward, stretching her hamstrings. But then he cradled her face in his palms. She'd never experienced this sort of connection with another person. It was more than sexual, it was a joining on all levels.

She feasted her gaze on him, watching his eyes become darker, more hooded. Droplets of sweat dotted his eyebrows, and his confident smile faded as he tipped back his head.

His cock swelled, and he moved faster, pulling out only a little before surging in again. He filled her completely, and that realization drove her response.

"So fucking...you're mine." He fisted his hands into her hair, holding her tight as he ejaculated, repeating her name over and over.

Even in the throes and aftermath of sex, he took care not to collapse on top of her. Instead, he braced himself near her shoulders, and he looked at her, as if memorizing her face.

"Everything about you is perfect."

She swallowed deeply. Whatever *this* was, it was making her an emotional wreck. She smiled to cover her confusion.

Long moments later, he adjusted her on the bed so that her body was completely supported by the mattress. Only then did he leave her to dispose of the condom.

He was back within seconds, joining her, holding her. "You did amazingly well."

"You make it easy." She turned onto her side and snuggled

up against the lean, protective planes of his body. His reactions ensured she wasn't self-conscious, giving her freedom to explore.

Entwined, they fell into silence. Eureka rang his bell and told himself he was a pretty bird.

Trace grinned. "He's got a healthy ego."

"I think all the males around here do."

Her body began to cool, and her muscles, unaccustomed to being stretched so far, began to burn a little. "I think I'll take a bath."

"Make it a shower and I'll join you."

CHAPTER EIGHT

HAWKEYE

T race was navigating foreign territory.

Even with Monica, he'd always been able to separate the strands of the relationship and BDSM. He was her Dom. She was a sub. They had cared for each other for a time, and yet he had never been obsessed with her. He never lost sleep because of an argument.

Yet he couldn't stop thinking about Aimee, how to please her, give her new experiences, while protecting her. Not just physically, but emotionally.

It disturbed him.

Maybe it was the constant proximity, the responsibility. Even the knowledge Inamorata was depending on him to stay sharp and keep Aimee safe.

And maybe it was something damn else entirely.

After checking the security system and his phone, he made his rounds through the house again. It was unnecessary, but still a compulsion.

In the dining room, Eureka growled at him. Confounding avian. At times, they were friends. Of course, the bird had probably heard Aimee's cries, maybe making him territorial.

The feathered pet lifted one of his feet and stared at Trace.

"I'm glad you're in the cage." He grabbed a nut from a bowl as a pseudo peace offering. Eureka moved to bite him with his ferocious bill. "I've heard parrot tastes like chicken."

"Tastes like chicken."

Sure everything was safe, he headed back to join Aimee.

The room was steamy and smelled of lavender, or what he thought might be lavender. Could have been any flower, he supposed, even rose or lilac. Regardless, it smelled fresh, feminine, and appealing, just the way a sub of his should smell.

His cock was hard again, and he hadn't even looked at her yet. He stripped and dropped his clothes in the hamper with hers. He didn't think too long or too hard about what that meant. It just seemed more respectful than dumping them on the floor. Or that was what he told himself.

He slid back the shower door, and she looked up at him. Water dripped from her hair, and several drops clung to her long eyelashes. She held on to a round nylon-looking thing that was oozing lather.

"I can't say that a man has ever been in the shower with me before."

"I like being your first." He entered the shower and then reached to cup her breasts. He loved the dark, dusky pink of her small nipples and how quickly they hardened when he gently pinched them. She moaned, her knees going forward a bit. "Tell me how much pressure you like. How much feels like too much? How much pushes you past that point and makes your pussy throb?"

"Even your words do that to me," she admitted.

He tightened his grip a little.

Her mouth opened.

"You like that?"

"Oh. Yes. Yes."

He applied a bit more pressure, and her eyes closed. Even more and she gasped, panting. "That?"

"Hurts," she whispered.

"And this?"

She cried out.

"You didn't just come, did you?"

She blinked. Then she laughed nervously. "I guess that's the point where my pussy throbs."

"Did you come without permission, *querida*?"

"I guess I need to be punished."

Dios. Save him.

"Will you punish me, Trace?"

This time, she took an assertive role, and he was about done for.

She raised onto her tiptoes, dropped the poufy thing, then wrapped her arms around his neck. She leaned into him, pulling his head downward so she could kiss him.

Where he was demanding, she was a bit more tentative, but when he opened his mouth for her, she took a bit more of an aggressive role, finding his tongue, then retreating.

He liked the way she tasted. It was more than that. It was about her willingness to please him, her desire to make him want her in return.

His dick throbbed against the softness of her belly.

She pulled away a little, long enough to look him in the eyes, and against his mouth, quietly said, "I love the sight of your cock."

Where the hell was his sweet, innocent submissive?

She folded a soapy hand around his cock and began to stroke him. As hard as he was for her, it would take her less than a dozen strokes to jerk him off. Half a dozen if... "Aimee!" He grabbed her hand.

117

She increased her pressure and made the strokes faster and shorter. Dios. He tightened his grip, forcing her to stop.

"Do you like that, Trace? *Sir*?"

How in the name of sweet Jesus did he go from being in charge to being bewitched? "I didn't give you permission to touch me."

"I didn't ask for it." She bit his lower lip. Hard. "I wanted to touch you. And I want to suck you as well."

Had she used one of her mosquitoes when he was outside, planting something inside him that told her exactly what he wanted and how he wanted it? Something had definitely gotten under his skin. "You want me? It's more than mutual, but we'll do it my way. Face the wall, Aimee." He liked her shower. It was big enough for both of them, with room to maneuver. She'd obviously spared no expense here. The showerhead was oversize, and it was adjustable, height wise. The interior was tiled, with a built-in bench, something he was certain they would take advantage of when he got around to letting her suck him, something that, if he thought about it too long, would make him come at the first skin-to-skin contact.

She turned while he picked up the bottle of body soap from a shelf. "Hands on the wall," he instructed. "Above your head." Her sweetheart of an ass was temptation manifested. If he weren't careful, he'd forget he was supposed to be the Dom here.

He squirted some of the soap into his palm as he looked at the bottle. Lilac, not lavender. He'd been close. At least they were both purple flowers. He lathered both hands and smoothed them over her shoulders, then down her back. She gave a small moan that made his cock stretch and strain even harder.

Then he bent behind her. "Feet at shoulder width, Aimee."

She slowly moved into position.

Water ran over both of them, and this close to her, he inhaled the smell of her. It was all he could do not to bury himself there, all he could do not to lick her until she came all over his mouth.

He soaped her legs one at a time and adjusted the showerhead to rinse her completely. He cleaned the soap from his hands before stroking between her legs. Her pussy was slick from her own juices, and she needed no lubrication.

He moved his forefinger back and forth across her clit. Then he brought in his other hand to spread her labia and pull back the hood of her clit. It amazed him how much he liked to touch her. The sound of her pleasure spiked his own. He wasn't generally into self-denial, but this woman made him want her pleasure more than he wanted his own.

She jerked and gave that tiny moan that he recognized as a precursor to her orgasm. She was so responsive, so easy to please. He gave her clit a tiny pinch. She gasped, her forehead falling forward to hit the tile.

The tiny pinch had interrupted her orgasm, and he easily slid a finger inside her.

Her breaths were shortened, little bursts of air, and he slipped in a second finger beside the first. "More?" he asked.

He saw her fingers splay above her head. "Yes," she whispered.

"Tell me."

"I want another finger inside me."

He finger fucked her until she rocked back and forth. It was hard not to get caught up in her reactions. In his less experienced years, he would have taken her while she was in a heated frenzy. But he wanted her over and over again, wanted her satisfaction, wanted her to enjoy all the experiences he could give her. More than ever, this was about her, testing her limits, taking her places she hadn't known existed. That he got to go there with her was just pleasure on top of pleasure.

"Trace," she whispered. "Trace. I want… I'm going to come."

He had guessed that a fraction of a second before she said anything. He stopped his motions, gently pulling out of her. She gave a halfhearted cry of protest but didn't say anything else. Trace adjusted the water, making sure it fell warmly on her body. Then he continued to soothe her until she quit shaking from the second denied orgasm. "I'm proud of you," he said.

"I didn't want you to stop."

"Yeah. I gathered that."

"You really are a sadist."

"A happy one, since I found an avowed masochist to play with."

"Beast," she said, stamping her right foot.

"Just think how spectacular your first anal orgasm will be."

She froze.

"Relax." He drew some of the arousal from her pussy back toward her anal whorl.

"Nervous," she said with a little laugh. "I tried before. It was a disaster."

"I want you to trust me. I won't do anything you're uncomfortable with. We'll start with one finger, like we just did. And only when you're ready for a second will I attempt it."

"No sex?"

"Not until you're ready." He leaned in very close as he touched a finger to her most private area.

She nodded.

"When I push in, bear down and push your anal muscles back against me."

"You're serious?"

He took her earlobe in his mouth and gently bit. Then he trailed kisses down the column of her throat to distract her.

He felt her relax slightly, and he stroked her pussy with featherlight motions even as he put a small amount of pressure on her anus. "You're doing great," he said.

"You haven't done anything yet."

He brought his left hand up to cup her breast, and then he pinched a nipple. She yelped and arched her back as she tried to evade him. He took the opportunity to effortlessly enter her rear.

"Damn!"

He kissed the top of her head. "You're there," he told her.

"I've been scared of *that?*"

"'Fraid so."

She sighed exaggeratedly.

"Not so bad?"

"It's amazing."

He moved his finger, stretching her a bit.

"I… Er…" She wiggled her hips experimentally. "I think I like that."

He couldn't wait to take her this way, filling her ass with his cock, driving it home, making her scream as she came. "I hoped you would."

"Can you…? Will you try a second?"

"I'd prefer to use lube for that."

"There's some in the cabinet under the sink."

"Was that a please?"

"I want a second finger up my ass. Please."

He laughed. Quick study. She exceeded all his hopes, and he had had very high hopes. "Greedy little sub."

"I said please."

He left her for a moment, dripping water all over the floor. The lube was conveniently at the front of the extra toiletries and her lotion. He grabbed the bottle, flipping open the lid and squirting a dollop onto his fingertips before he even returned to the shower.

She was in the same position where he'd left her, even with her legs spread, waiting. At this point, she could lead him around by his cock, and he'd follow her anywhere.

He backed up a bit instead of starting from where they'd left off. Even without his telling her, she arched her back for him. He wrapped one arm around her.

"Will you stroke my pussy?"

"Ask nice. Like a sub."

"Sir… Trace… Will you please stroke my pussy?"

Fuck. "Happy to." He did. Simultaneously he pressed a finger against her rear entrance.

She thrust back against him.

"Old pro," he said. He kissed the side of her neck. He couldn't help himself, not because he thought it would please her, but because he wanted to. He wanted her to be his, and he wanted to mark her. He wouldn't actually do it, but damn it, he wanted to.

This surge of possessiveness was odd. In the past, he'd sometimes shared his subs, but the idea of sharing her pissed him off.

He moved his finger in and out. Then, when he thought she was ready, he brought a second finger up beside the first and eased both inside her.

She gasped. "That's a little more challenging," she said. "You've got big fingers."

Her breaths were a little close together, as if she might be close to freaking out. He stroked her clit just a little faster.

"That… Yes. Right. There."

"You like it?"

"Feeling overwhelmed," she admitted. "It hurts. But…" Then she screamed.

Her orgasm surprised him, and if he didn't guess wrong, it surprised her as well. He caught her as she collapsed backward into him.

"I'm sorry. I know I'm not supposed to do that."

"That one's a freebie. You earned it."

"No punishment?"

He wiped the water from her eyes as she tipped back her head.

"That's fair," she said when he didn't respond. "It was your fault, anyway."

"Is it indeed?"

"Well, if you weren't such a skillful lover, I could have held on longer."

"Do we need to have a discussion about personal responsibility?" How long, if ever, since he'd teased a woman?

"No, Sir." She batted her eyelashes.

Yeah, she could lead him anywhere.

"I think it's time for your butt plug."

"I'm not sure I'm ready."

"You will be." Keeping her supported, he pulled first one, then the other finger, from her rear.

She wiggled about until she faced him, then pushed runaway strands of hair back from her face.

He turned off the faucet and reached for one of the towels she'd thrown over the shower door. After drying her hair and her face and trailing the towel down her neck and across her chest, he said, "Turn around."

Obediently, she did.

He ran the soft material across her shoulders, then down

her back, before rubbing the towel across her buttocks. He crouched to dry her legs, before finally moving to her intimate parts. Her labia were swollen and reddened. If he'd ever seen anything more appealing, he didn't remember the sight. "Now the front." His voice was husky. If he didn't get her into the bedroom immediately, he'd take her right here in the shower.

After she was dry, he tossed the damp towel back on top of the door and snagged the other for himself. "Wait for me in the bedroom."

She inhaled, but showed no sign of protesting. Aimee started to pass him but paused. She reached up and stroked his chin with the back of her hand. "You turn me on."

"Yeah?" She left the room, and for far too long, he watched her. Then, shaking his head, he gave his body a cursory pass with the towel before following her.

Aimee was lying on top of the bed on her side, her head propped on her upturned arm. From earlier, the lube and the plug were on top of the nightstand. "I want you on your stomach, with a pillow beneath it."

Her eyes widened as she followed his gaze. "You're going to put the plug in?"

"Another time I'll watch you do it. But yes, I plan to put it in you. Now roll over."

She followed his instructions, her knees digging into the mattress. He put one knee on the mattress, near her, and then he liberally covered the stainless steel with lube. "Keep your legs apart." He placed the narrow teardrop-shaped tip against her opening. She was lovely in her submission, and the sight of her completely exposed made his cock throb. "This won't hurt a bit."

She laughed, enough to loosen the tension, and he seized the moment. With a swift, sure motion, he sank it all the way in.

She gasped, and her hips jerked, but she settled almost instantly. "It's cold," she said.

"Dios. That looks beautiful. I may just always keep your ass full."

She squirmed.

"And maybe we'll get you a bigger plug, one that stretches you even wider."

She turned her head to look at him. "You're serious?"

"Maybe a glass one."

"You're scaring me," she said. "Again."

Her voice was breathless. He enjoyed that about her. There was a quality to her voice when fear and trepidation melded into trust. It did strange things to him, appealed to his masculinity, made him want to protect her. He stroked blonde strands of hair back from her face. "You'll beg me for it, querida."

"A glass plug?" She turned her head to the side, straining her neck so she could look at him. "I'm going to beg for that?"

"You will," he promised. He wiggled the stainless plug he'd just inserted, tugging on it, then sinking it back in. "Do you like that?"

"I do. A lot. More than I thought I would." With a sigh, she whispered, "Fuck me?"

"I thought you'd never ask." He helped her onto her back before grabbing a condom. It seemed to take longer than ever to rip open the packet and roll the latex down the length of his shaft.

"I like to look at your cock, Sir."

He grinned. "I like to have you look at it." He moved between her legs, poised at the entrance to her pussy. "And touch it."

"Do you enjoy this?" She showed him what she meant, closing her hand around him tightly.

"Yeah."

She stroked him, slowly at first, then more vigorously.

His head fell forward. Control threatened to fracture. Propping his weight on one arm, he curled his other hand around hers, stopping her motions. "I want you to jerk me off," he said. "Later. Right now I want to be inside you while your ass is full of that plug."

"Take me."

He needed no second invitation.

She was already wet, and he slid in the first inch effortlessly.

"I can feel the plug," she said. "It…"

"You okay?"

She inhaled sharply. "Yes." Then again, more surely, she said, "Yes."

He entered deeper. Despite the fact that they'd had sex earlier, she was still tight, and the size of the plug made the fit feel even more snug. He forced himself to grit his teeth and pace his strokes, not giving in to her whimpered urgings or his own body's demands.

He grabbed her wrists and imprisoned them above her head. He loved the way they looked together, his darker skin contrasting with her much lighter tone, his strength complementing her femininity, his dominance made more complete by her sweet submission.

Because he was already on the verge of orgasm, Trace withdrew. He took a moment to recover so he could stay in control, pacing himself while he heightened her arousal to the point where her world would shatter. He pulled one of her nipples into his mouth, biting it with more pressure than he'd used before.

"Trace! That's…"

"Too much?"

"Fantastic."

He moved to her other nipple, giving it the same intense attention.

Her head thrashed back and forth, and the sight of her capitulation drove him to the edge. He thrust back into her, riding her hard, wanting her to experience the madness that consumed him.

"I want to come."

"Beg," he told her. "Beg."

"Please? Please, Trace. I can't…" She whimpered. "I can't take any more."

"A few more seconds." Her body convulsed beneath him. "Now." He sank his teeth into her shoulder.

She screamed. Her body bucked and trembled. Not for the first time, he thought of how perfect she was for him, strong enough to offer everything he demanded, soft enough to yield to his needs.

After she came, he rode out his own orgasm. He bit out a curse in Spanish. Each climax he had with her was more wrenching than the previous one.

When he finally opened his eyes, she was looking up at him. The color of her eyes was lighter than he had ever seen before. Her mouth was open slightly. Her blonde hair was mussed all over her face. And he was ensnared, as surely as if she'd slapped a pair of unyielding metal handcuffs on him.

After he disposed of the condom, she snuggled against him and drifted off to sleep. He could, maybe should, get up. Instead, he held her. He didn't question the rightness of having her body pressed against his so trustingly. Nor did he question his own determination to keep her safe.

Maybe a half hour later, he climbed from the bed and went to the living room to dig out a pair of shorts and a fresh T-shirt from his duffel. He had a hard time concentrating on what he was doing.

He skipped socks and stuffed his feet into his running shoes.

After grabbing his gun, he walked through the house, then went into the kitchen. That damn bird growled again. "Tastes like chicken," Trace said before heading outside to check in with the team.

AIMEE SAT UP IN BED AND WRAPPED HER ARMS AROUND HER upturned knees, very much aware of the plug still deep inside her.

Dozens of emotions crashed over her.

She was used to sleeping alone, and she liked her sleep, eight hours at a minimum, preferably nine, and on rare occasions, a full ten. This was the first time she'd woken up feeling lonely.

Trace wouldn't have gone far, but she didn't hear him moving around. The bedside lamp was still on from earlier, but the rest of the house was dark. Was he on the couch, abandoning her after their hot sex? Had it meant something to her, but not to him?

As silence became more familiar, she became aware of the sound of voices outside. Not just his but others, likely one of the security teams. It reminded her that he had a job to do.

He might fulfill her deepest sexual fantasies, but the moment the assignment ended, he'd move on, maybe to the wilds of a jungle or perhaps a Middle East war zone. She would still be in Denver, Colorado, continuing her work, teaching classes, running every day...alone, remembering him, wondering what he was doing, *who* he was doing...

Trace had been right to question whether or not they should get involved. Maybe she'd been overly confident in her ability to keep her emotions out of the relationship. And perhaps she'd never met anyone like him before. "Damn. Damn, damn, damn. *Damn.*"

She swiped away her sudden, stinging tears. Aimee Inamorata was not the kind of woman who felt sorry for herself. Her older sister had made sure of that. Following the death of their parents and then the horrible incident that had happened to her in college, she had become more resolute than ever, taking self-defense classes and learning to shoot a gun. Then, to prove events didn't define who she was, the older Inamorata had learned to shoot a gun, and joined Hawkeye. She'd insisted that Aimee should be confident in her life, too.

Despite her inner resolve, she wasn't sure what to do about Trace. The reactions he'd wrung from her when she submitted left her exposed, emotionally vulnerable.

She exhaled shakily.

Being involved with Jack had been devastating. But this could destroy her.

The front door closed and the lock turned, jolting her. Aimee steeled her resolve. She had to keep her emotions walled off from him, no matter how difficult.

He returned to the bedroom smelling of the cool Colorado evening and the tang of seduction.

"Didn't mean to wake you, querida."

"You didn't. Not really. I wasn't aware of your leaving the bed, but when I turned and you weren't there…"

"I'm back. I'll always come back." He crossed the room and toed off his shoes. He smoothed her hair back from her face. It amazed her how tender he could be. "How are you feeling? Is the plug okay?"

"Surprisingly, yes."

"Since you're awake, I'll give you two choices of how we can spend our time."

Her heart picked up a few extra beats.

"Bent over? From behind?" He held her head between his hands and leaned forward to kiss her and her response was immediate, proving how difficult it would be to keep her distance from him.

He drew her lower lip between his teeth, then used his tongue to coax her into opening her mouth. Then he deepened the kiss, probing, seeking. She could have no secrets from him.

Silently communicating his urgency, Trace ended the kiss. After putting the gun on the nightstand, he dropped his clothes. "I can't get enough of you," he admitted, his voice as hoarse as her own. "Take my hand." As she did, he eased her from the bed. Once she was standing, he instructed, "I want you right there." He pointed to a spot about a foot away.

"Facing you?" she asked when she was in place.

"For now. Spread your legs…as wide as you can."

She did, and he knelt in front of her. Aimee shivered. Big, strong, powerful Trace Romero was on his knees, with his mouth at her crotch level.

"Just making sure you're ready."

"I'm ready!"

He looked up at her, capturing her gaze. Then he leaned in and licked her pussy.

"I'm ready, Sir." It would only take seconds for her to come undone. That was probably his diabolical plan. Wring an orgasm from her, then punish her for it.

She grabbed his shoulders, trying to keep her balance. When he did…*that*…she could hardly hold herself up.

He spread her labia with one hand. With the other, he toyed with her plug.

"Ready," she repeated, gasping through gritted teeth. "Really, really ready."

He kept at it, licking her pussy, changing the amount of pressure on her clit. His touch was magic. He slipped his tongue inside her while he gave a particularly firm tug on her plug. Her whole body was on fire.

She moved her hands, digging her fingers into his hair.

He pulled out the plug even farther, then shoved it in. She was done for.

She screamed as she shattered.

He kept up his maddening motions, dragging a second orgasm from her.

"Now," he said, looking up at her and grinning, "you're ready. I'm glad you're so fit," he said. "It'll make it easier for you to stay in position."

She turned her back to him, and he trailed his fingers down her spine, then into the crack of her rear. Every nerve ending was being singed. This man knew how to touch her, where to touch her, and for how long to touch her.

He grabbed a condom, then moved in behind her to press his cockhead against her pussy. Her breaths came closer and closer together, even though he'd barely started to touch her.

"So hot," he murmured. "Hot." He grabbed her hips and held her tight as he pushed inexorably forward.

"It feels…different than anything else has." It had to be the combination of the position and the fact that she was a little out of control. The blood rush to her head only enhanced the intensity.

He grunted, and she took silent pleasure from the fact that he was turned on. It was something that she had some sort of power over him.

Trace dragged her backward and managed to snake his arm around her middle so he could hold her completely imprisoned while he fucked her. Having him so totally in charge allowed her to shove away her fears and let go. She felt his orgasm building before she heard his deep groan of appreciation.

He held her, and he pounded into her. His cock was hard, pulsing.

She wanted his orgasm as much as he previously demanded hers. He dug his fingers into her, no doubt leaving tiny bruises that she wanted. Finally, when her body was exhausted, he shuddered, climaxing hard, slamming into her.

Aimee expected him to pull away, but he reached around and fingered her while he still had her pussy filled. The intensity of the angle combined with his unyielding and relentless pressure on her clit made her tremble. "You don't need to do this."

"Don't fight me." His words were a demand.

He still held her, and he made his movements shorter and more intense.

"Come, Aimee." He slapped her pussy.

The orgasm plowed into her, buckling her knees. He tightened his hold, supporting her closer, letting her know he wouldn't let her go.

Long moments later, he withdrew. Since she was wobbly, he helped her to the bed.

"Stay there," he said.

She wasn't capable of going anywhere for a very long time, even if he were to order it.

A minute later he returned and pressed a warm, damp washcloth to her pussy.

"Relax."

She closed her eyes, enjoying the small luxury. After soothing her clit and gently wiping her, he used the small cotton towel to remove the plug. She exhaled. "Thank you."

He crawled in behind her and pulled her close, settling his cock between her ass cheeks before pulling blankets over them both.

"I think I might like this submissive stuff."

"You think?"

"Maybe," she said teasingly. "I may need a little more experience to know for sure."

He reached around and tweaked one of her nipples.

She yelped.

"Then tomorrow, I'll give you another lesson, and we'll see how that goes. You can let me know then how it's working for you."

CHAPTER NINE

HAWKEYE

offee. Coffee would be good. Her usual fix of an extra-
large vanilla soy latte would be even better.

Aimee dragged a pillow over her head to block out the
bright late-summer Rocky Mountain sunshine.

Reality slowly returned, and she became aware of the
tenderness between her legs and the fact that her nipples
were slightly sore.

She rolled over and pushed up onto one elbow. She saw
the indentation on the pillow Trace had used. Even without
that, she would know it hadn't been a dream. The scent of
him lingered in the room. A discarded T-shirt hung from one
of the bedposts. His presence dominated the space, even
though he wasn't in it.

A pot clattered in the kitchen.

Then Eureka chimed in. "Get up. Get up!"

Aimee slowly realized that coffee wasn't just a dream or a
need. The richness of its brewing scent had awakened her.
She could get used to someone more ambitious than she was
getting out of bed and brewing the first pot.

She'd always considered the idea of having someone in

her space to be detrimental. But then, she'd never put together an official pros-and-cons list on the idea of living with someone. Until Trace, there had been no point. Being put to bed and awakened by the scent of coffee could potentially outrank ten negatives, like doing someone else's laundry.

"Morning." Trace stood in the doorway, his shoulder propped against the jamb. He held a steaming cup of coffee in hand. Her mouth watered, and not just from anticipation of her own cup of coffee, but from the sight of him.

He smelled fresh, of spicy soap, citrusy shampoo, and first-of-the-morning air.

Black T-shirts were made for him, and he could have walked out of a magazine ad for those blue jeans. Just open the top button and…

Aimee sat up, dragging the sheet with her. She tucked her hair back as he studied her, as if he intended to know all of her secrets.

He entered the room and sat on the edge of the bed. Even from yesterday, their level of intimacy had changed. It wasn't just her bedroom…it was theirs.

She accepted the proffered drink and took a long sip. "Thank you."

"Drop the sheet."

Instead of waiting for her to comply, he captured the high-thread-count cotton and pulled it away from her body. Her nipples hardened instantly, in response to the room's chill and the heat of his gaze.

"I'd keep you naked all day if it were up to me." He cupped her left breast gently, and dampness flooded between her legs. "Careful with the coffee."

He was a master. He had her exactly where he wanted her, as usual.

Watching her intently, he pinched her nipple between his thumb and forefinger and continued until she gasped.

"You are so amazing to play with," he said. He tweaked her nipple one final time. "Get dressed. Breakfast awaits."

She blinked the world back into focus. "Breakfast?"

"The meal between dinner and lunch."

"You're leaving me like this?"

"I like my subs hungry in all ways." With only a glance over his shoulder, he exited the room.

She sank against the headboard to collect herself, once again. Resisting him was easy when it was a theory, another when he was in her space, breathing the same air as she was.

After a few sips of the hot brew, she climbed out of bed. She'd never before woken up naked. In summer, she generally slept in long shirts, and she had a few favorites, several with pictures of Einstein along with some of his more famous quotes, a couple bearing the likeness of Richard Feynman, and a purple one from Neil deGrasse Tyson's recent tour. Some women went to rock concerts. She attended science lectures.

Reminding herself that she needed to keep her emotions safe from him, she dressed in jeans and a T-shirt.

The scene in the kitchen shocked her. Trace stood in front of the stove, his back to her as he sang in Spanish. She could get used to that, she decided. Any man who could operate a paring knife, a frying pan, a toaster, and a coffee maker, all in the same morning, was her hero.

But it wasn't only that.

Eureka stood on top of his cage, his foot wrapped around a slice of apple. He glanced at Trace occasionally, but that Trace had let the bird out of the cage and fed him… It was doubly difficult to keep her distance.

"Thank you."

He turned to face her. "For the coffee?"

"Mainly for Eureka," she said.

"I figured I should plump him up, put some meat on his bones, before we roast him for dinner."

"Bombs away!"

She looked over her shoulder and pointed at the bird. "Eureka, no."

He picked up the piece of apple that he'd discarded.

"Tastes like chicken," Eureka repeated. "Tastes like chicken."

"Oh my God, Trace. What have you been saying to him when I'm not around?"

"I thought it was a private conversation."

"Bombs away!"

She glared at the bird again, but he was eating, obviously having made his point. "What's for breakfast?"

"Omelets," he said, reaching for a spatula. "With avocados and cream cheese. I also made fresh salsa."

"I mean it, if the security, gun-carrying thing doesn't work out, you're welcome to apply for a job with me."

His eyes darkened. "I've got a different proposition in mind." Before she could react, he had dropped the spatula and had her against the counter. His right leg was between hers, her crotch against his thigh. He dug his hand into her hair, holding her captive for his kiss.

She wrapped her arms around his neck and responded completely. She had no resistance where he was concerned. As he'd obviously intended, she moved her pussy against his leg while he devoured her mouth in a demanding kiss.

Even though she'd had half a dozen orgasms last night, another was right there, gnawing at her.

He moved his free hand to her lower back, and the pressure he exerted changed her position a bit, bringing her in more firm contact with his leg. He had to know what he was doing, had to know its effect on her…

She came, hard, and with a whimper that was muffled against his mouth.

"Now," he said, "it's a good morning."

When her head stopped spinning, she nodded. It was.

"Set the table before I burn breakfast."

While she put colorful place mats on the table, she kept glancing at him. He was more than competent in the kitchen. He was at home. It frightened her, more than just a little bit, to realize how comfortable she was with him here. "More coffee?" She offered the drink as if having a man in her kitchen at this time of the morning were the most natural thing in the world.

"Black," he said. "Although after tasting the cream on your kiss, I'm tempted to have you put some in mine."

She refilled his mug, then grabbed herself a new one from the cupboard, adding a huge dollop of half-and-half.

He brought two plates to the table, and after she took the first bite, she sighed. The flavors melded on her tongue, complemented by the bite from the jalapenos in the salsa. "Trace, this is amazing. Thank you."

After breakfast, he said, "Are you working today?"

"I thought I'd get in a couple of hours and then go get a latte?"

He nodded.

Some semblance of normalcy...and keeping them out of the bedroom. "And a run this afternoon?"

He nodded. "Go to work. I'll take care of this."

Her cell phone rang, and she went to answer it while Trace cleared the dishes. When she heard her sister's voice, she said, "I've been offered half the money in the pot if I just cough up your name. I hear there's enough for a nice trip to the Bahamas."

"Won't matter if I kill you. You have to be alive to enjoy the trip."

"That's what I was afraid of." Aimee laughed, but her sister didn't. Her body chilled. "Something's wrong."

"I'm going to talk to Agent Romero, but I wanted to speak with you first. He'll have some instructions for you, and you need to follow them."

"What happened?"

"Aimee—"

"I need to know."

For a moment, she was silent. Then, in her normal no-nonsense way, she said, "Jason Knoll was found dead."

Aimee dropped into a chair.

"I don't have many details. I'll pass along anything I find out."

Trace was already walking over to take the phone from her. Numb, from the inside out, she gave him the handset. He strode to the patio door, and she retreated to her office.

She powered up her computer, then logged into the system. Within seconds, messages flooded her screen with the news that they'd lost Jason.

How was it even possible? Just yesterday he'd been alive and vibrant at Hawkeye headquarters. In silence, she stared at the screen, unblinking.

Trace knocked on her doorjamb before entering the room.

"He was there, yesterday. You saw him. The one with the long hair, the ridiculous colored T-shirt."

"Bare feet?"

"Yeah. Always. Kind of a trademark."

He came up behind her, then gently spun her chair so that she faced him. "I'm sorry, querida." With amazing tenderness, he took her by the shoulders and helped her from the chair.

She sank her head onto his chest, and he wrapped his arms around her, holding her tight, sharing his strength. For a long time, she stayed there, protected, and he said nothing, maybe guessing that she didn't want to hear anything meaningless or trite. He simply offered his support. "Jason wasn't even twenty," she said. She tried to swallow the lump in her throat, and she valiantly blinked back the tears swimming in her eyes. "He was funny. Genius. Wanted to make the world a better place."

For long moments, Trace stroked her hair, saying nothing. Memories of Jason flashed through her mind in a random, senseless order. She continued to lean on Trace, to inhale his scent and draw from his steadiness. How had he become so important to her, so fast? "Did they get any of his work?"

"Inamorata believes so. His computer is missing."

She pulled back so she could study Trace's features, appreciating that he didn't try to lie to her or soften the news. Grief collided with reality. "Then the rest of us will have to work doubly hard to get the project finished."

"We're moving you."

"What? No." She shook her head, pushing away from him. "We need to finish the project. It's more important than ever."

"You'll be able to continue your work. But this isn't negotiable, Aimee." Steel made his voice implacable.

"Think about it. There are dozens of people on the team. You can't keep everyone safe. We just need to get it finished."

"You're my responsibility. The one who matters to me."

"Wait… I can't. I need to think. Some space. Time."

"You've got thirty minutes," he said. "I'd prefer you get ready in twenty."

"Trace—"

"Take it up with your sister. Or Hawkeye. I have my orders. And we will be out of this house in half an hour or less, Aimee. Whether you're ready or not."

She stared at him. "There's too many considerations. Eureka?"

"Can one of your neighbors—"

"Don't even go there, Agent." If he was going to withdraw, so was she. "If I go, so does he."

"It's not practical to haul a parrot—"

"You're not listening."

He sighed. "You've got twenty-nine minutes. We're headed to the mountains, so bring a jacket."

"Don't I get any say in this?"

Without replying, he left the room.

She resisted her immediate impulse to drop back into her chair and interact with her colleagues, friends. People who would understand the magnitude of the loss.

Instead, she pulled back her shoulders and forced herself to focus, creating a mental checklist of everything she needed.

After powering down her computer, she loaded it into her backpack, along with power cables. Then she hurried into the master bathroom to pack toiletries. *Focus.* She fetched a suitcase from the closet, then grabbed workout clothes, jeans, T-shirts, hiking boots, running shoes, sweatshirts, a jacket, and a pair of gloves.

The front door closed, and a car engine hummed.

Trace joined her in the bedroom a few minutes later. He was dressed in a long-sleeved T-shirt, and if she wasn't mistaken, there was a radio beneath it. "Are you getting close?"

"Not sure I thought of everything."

"We can have someone bring it to you."

"Okay." She nodded, trying to slow down her tumbling thoughts. "Eureka's travel cage is in the office closet. And he'll need fresh fruit. Nuts. His regular food also."

"I'll handle it."

"Thanks." Aimee double-checked all the things she'd packed, added some warm pajamas, then zipped her suitcase. She slung her backpack over her shoulders and wheeled the luggage toward the front door.

Trace was in the dining room, and Eureka was hiding in his regular cage, against the far side, facing away from them. Most often, when they traveled, it was to the vet. It was no wonder he didn't want to cooperate.

"I'll start loading up."

As he turned away, she noticed the gun tucked into his waistband. She should be easier with this by now, but she wasn't. "Time to go for a ride, Eureka." Tamping down her stress so that she didn't make him more anxious, she slowly put her hand in the cage. "Step up."

He ignored her.

It took several minutes of coaxing to get him out of his cage and into the smaller one, and the entire time, she was aware of Trace's return and rising tension as the minutes ticked past.

"Ready," she announced when Eureka was finally settled.

"You and I will be taking my vehicle. Eureka will ride in the backseat. Agent Laurents is waiting on the porch. Barstow will get you settled. They'll travel behind us. Riley and Mallory will be in front of us. This needs to happen as fast as possible. Any questions?"

Swimming in a surreal sea, she shook her head.

"Are you okay carrying the cage?"

Which probably meant he wanted his hands free. "It's not a problem."

"Ready?"

She unclenched her hands in an attempt to relax. "Let's roll."

"Whee!" Eureka cried out when she picked up the cage.

He lifted his hand and pressed a button on his high-tech

watch. "Falcon's on the move." With a tight nod, he opened the front door.

"Ma'am," Laurents greeted, falling in step next to her.

Barstow stood near the tanklike SUV, and the doors were already open. Both men wore long-sleeve black shirts, black pants, and boots, and no personal items. They were both within an inch height wise, with dark hair, brown eyes, and athletic builds.

As she approached, Barstow extended his hand for the birdcage. "If he can go on the floor, it might be more secure," she said.

"Of course, Miss Inamorata."

She reached for a strap to pull herself up into the front seat, and Laurents sealed her in.

Trace jumped in next to her, gave her a quick once-over, made sure Eureka was situated, then told Barstow, "Clear."

"Yes, sir."

As the door slammed, Trace dropped the transmission into drive and accelerated out of the driveway.

Close to the end of the street, a vehicle pulled in front of them, and a check in the side view mirror showed that Barstow and Laurents were already on their tail. "I'm freaking out a little," she admitted as he rolled through a four-way stop without slowing down.

"Good." He glanced at her. "A little I can deal with. Nerves will keep you sharp. We need that."

Tension hung thick in the compartment as they drove, and Trace's grip on the steering wheel only loosened when they were on I-70, west of Denver where the traffic thinned out. Even Eureka had been silent, as if he understood the urgency. "Am I allowed to know where we're going?"

"My family's cabin. It's between Granby and Grand Lake."

"Oh?"

"My father built it right after they had their first kid, in the early days of their marriage. He wanted a place for the family to gather, keep us all close. Get away from the heat of a Texas summer."

"Sounds nice." The response was automatic, not thought out.

"It is. We try to get up there every year, still. Not all of us at once, but it's nice to know it's always there." He checked his speed and the mirrors before speaking again. "Your sister has rented a couple of other cabins in the area so the operatives can be close, and so that we can limit the number of people legitimately in the area. She's arranged to have the refrigerator stocked."

"This feels like I'm suddenly living someone else's life."

"It's difficult, and I'm so fucking proud of you."

She turned slightly so she could look at him. "Proud of me?"

"You've kept it together when most wouldn't be able to. You're doing good."

He took the exit for Winter Park, slowed down through Empire, then began navigating the harrowing twists and turns of Berthoud Pass. On some days, the view went on forever, but today, low clouds obscured the view. It was fitting.

At least an hour later, he turned off the pavement onto a dirt road. Eureka squawked.

"Sorry, guy," she told him. "Has to be a rough trip in a cage."

"It's going to get worse," Trace said by way of apology as he followed the SUV that Riley was driving.

"Aimee! Aimee!" Eureka protested as the vehicle traversed the bumpy road.

"Almost there." She was gritting her teeth by the time Trace pulled off the bumpy road and slowed to crawl up what appeared to be a barely maintained driveway.

When she thought the trip would never end, a two-story cabin came into view. It was much bigger than she'd pictured, more of a second home than a weekend getaway, and it appeared to have been constructed from hand-hewn logs. The numbers next to the front door were painted on colorful Mexican tiles.

Off to the right side of the family home was a small grotto accented with wildflowers, with a red hummingbird feeder hanging from a pole. The nearby pine trees cast long, towering shadows.

Trace turned off the vehicle's engine but left the keys in the ignition. "Stay put until either I or one of the operatives comes for you."

She nodded and released the latch to the safety belt. He reached into the back to grab something, and Eureka growled.

"Who the hell taught him to do that?"

"I'm told that the owner who surrendered him also had a rottweiler."

"Get up. Get up," Eureka insisted.

"Five minutes," she promised.

After parking behind them, Laurents and Barstow each went around the back of the cabin in different directions. Trace headed into the house with Riley, while Bree Mallory, hand on the pistol strapped to her waist, stayed near Aimee.

A minute or so later, Riley emerged from the house, followed by Trace, whose shoulders were not as tense as they had been earlier.

At Trace's nod, Mallory opened Aimee's door. "I need to get Eureka."

Mallory looked to Trace for her orders.

"It's fine."

He stood guard while she grabbed the birdcage.

"We'll get everything else, Miss Inamorata."

"Thank you."

Mallory walked just behind Aimee into the house.

She surveyed the surroundings and decided to place the cage on the gigantic wood-carved dining room table.

Within minutes, Mallory and Riley had unloaded the vehicle and wished her a good day.

"I want to talk with the team," Trace said. "I'll be back in a few minutes."

When he left, the silence became a shroud. Not even a clock ticked in the background. The cabin was chilly, not surprising at this altitude.

Wrapping her arms around herself, she explored her temporary home.

Upstairs there were four bedrooms, all large. Two had sets of bunk beds. And the master had a nice ensuite bathroom.

Downstairs, the main cabin was very much open. A large stone fireplace with a pine mantelpiece dominated the space. There were plenty of wingback chairs, a couple of inviting overstuffed couches, and large windows—unfortunately with the blinds closed. If her guess was right, Trace would keep them that way.

Against one wall, a built-in bookcase held board games, dice, dominoes, and multiple decks of cards. Throughout the place were plenty of female touches, from the dried flowers in a brass water pitcher to the bright serape thrown over the arm of a chair. A colorful handblown glass bowl sat atop the woven runner on the dining room table. A few family photos hung on one wall. Some of the shots looked as if they'd been in their places of honor for years, and the frames were mainly wood, in bright primary colors, although a couple were constructed from hammered tin. Framed snapshots adorned almost every surface.

She wandered over for a closer look. One appeared somewhat recent and had been taken outside the cabin. Trace stood next to an older couple. His parents, no doubt. All the loving memories—holidays, birthdays—were such a contrast to her past, where her sister had struggled to support her.

Restless, she walked to the kitchen. As promised, the refrigerator was full. And there was a gigantic bowl overflowing with bite-size candy bars.

She filled Eureka's water and placed a few pieces of fruit in his bowl. He ignored them as he tried to walk onto her hand. "Get up!"

"In a while."

He needed time to adapt to the surroundings, and she wanted to be sure he was comfortable before letting him out.

As she powered up her computer, she was very much aware of the murmur of voices outside the cabin, with Trace's being the dominant one.

A few minutes later, there was silence again.

Bree Mallory entered the cabin. "Agent Romero asked me to hang out here for a while."

"Hang out? You mean babysit."

"Pretend I'm not here, ma'am."

"Where's Trace?"

"Checking out the other cabins, surveying the land. Since it's his family's property, he knows it better than anyone."

"Makes sense."

No matter how hard she tried to settle in to her work, she couldn't, not with Bree walking around, looking out the windows, fingering the grip of her gun. "There's candy in the kitchen." Then she remembered the agent didn't have a sweet tooth. "And other snacks. Nuts. Protein bars. Water. Soda."

"Candy? I'll take some for Riley." But she didn't. Instead, she jogged up the stairs to check out the rooms, banging doors open, boots echoing off the floors.

Pretend she wasn't there?

Aimee stared at her computer screen. Her colleagues' reactions were varied. Some were overwhelmed by grief and needed the connection of reaching out and talking about Jason. Others were nervous for themselves and their families, questioning every odd detail happening in their lives. A handful buried themselves in work.

A few minutes later, Bree came back down the stairs.

"I appreciate this," Aimee said.

"Pleasure, ma'am. Anything for Ms. Inamorata's sister."

"It doesn't start with the letter A."

"That's good to know." She grinned. "Not that I would ask."

"However much is in the pot, I hope you win. You deserve it for being up here."

Trace returned, and he excused Mallory.

"Remember the chocolate for Riley," Aimee said.

"Thank you, ma'am." Bree grabbed a couple of bars and tucked them into her pockets before leaving.

While Aimee worked—the best she could—Trace made lunch and carried it to her at the table. She absently took a few bites of the sandwich and moved the potato chips around the plate.

"You don't like it?"

"I'm just…" She looked up. "Distracted."

"I know. It's critical to keep up your food and rest, though."

"It's easier said than done."

"We don't know how long we'll be here, what to expect. The last thing you need is to be hungry or exhausted."

On so many levels, what he said made sense, but she couldn't force herself to eat anything else.

"I'll take the luggage upstairs."

Hearing an unspoken question in his tone, she cocked her head to one side.

"One bedroom or two?"

She couldn't imagine wanting to be alone. "One. If that's okay with you?"

"Yeah. Exactly what I was hoping for."

Midafternoon, she allowed Eureka out of the cage, and he spent a happy hour flying from surface to surface before she ordered him back to base. He sat on top of the cage and played with a small plastic cup that Trace provided as a toy.

Somehow, they made it through the day, and in early evening, he lit a fire, then they sat together on one of the couches. Another time, this would by an idyllic retreat.

"Coffee?" he offered.

"Wine?"

"You could. But with the risk level, I'd rather we skip it."

"I can't get away from it."

"It will be over eventually."

She held on to that.

For the next hour, he regaled her with tales of the siblings' adventures in the mountains, snowmobiling in winter, kayaking on Lake Granby in the summer, horseback riding near Shadow Mountain Lake, playing little putt golf in downtown Grand Lake.

Finally, exhausted, she excused herself.

"I'll be up in an hour or so. I want to go over the night-time sentry duty schedule."

Always the reminder of his focus on his duty.

After putting Eureka in his cage, she went upstairs, took a bath, then waited for Trace.

It was closer to two hours before the sound of his footfall echoed through the quiet. He showered before slipping into the bed.

"Trace?"

"I'm sorry. Did I wake you?"

"No. I was waiting."

He took her in his arms and held her close. "You're so damn brave, Aimee."

"I'm not so sure about that."

"I've seen it all. You can believe what I say."

"I want sex."

"Aimee…"

"I need the connection. Not tender. I want to be reminded we're alive."

"Yeah." He breathed out, as if understanding exactly what she was saying. "Then you'd better get naked." His tone was commanding, and response flooded through her.

"Yes, Trace."

She sat up, and he scooped her T-shirt off, then tugged her shorts down.

He stood and pulled off his thin sleep pants before offering his hand. She took it, trembling from his strength.

"On your knees, preciosa."

She cupped his balls with one hand, and she closed the other around his shaft, squeezing firmly before leaning in to suck the precum from his slit.

"Enough," he ordered, and the gravel in his voice made her grin. "Bend over the bed, Aimee."

He helped her up and moved her into the position he wanted her, with her body wide open, exposed to him, for him. "Wait there." He grabbed a condom from his wallet, then sheathed himself before trailing his finger down her spine. "I love seeing you like this." He toyed with her clit before sliding a finger against her pussy. "Love that you're already wet for me."

"Take me," she pleaded.

He placed his cockhead against her entrance, and she thrust back, urging him on.

"You're mine, Aimee."

He'd said so before, but this time, there was a bar of

possessive steel in the statement. He dug his fingers into her shoulders.

She lost track of time, of fear, of grief, and she was wrapped up only in him.

He wrung orgasm after orgasm from her, smacking her ass, filling the room with her whimpers and sighs and moans.

When he came inside her, his domination was complete. Aimee was his. Despite her best efforts and rationalizations, she'd fallen in love with Trace Romero.

As he shifted their positions so he could kiss her hard, she wondered how she'd ever survive him.

CHAPTER TEN

HAWKEYE

Something woke Trace.

Or rather, the absence of something.

He reached for his phone and checked the display. Blank.

Schooling his pulse, he turned on a lamp and double-checked the time. Fifteen minutes after midnight. There should have been a message from Bree Mallory. The team had signed up for three-hour shifts. Laurents had taken six to nine. Riley had relieved him. Then Mallory was on until three, followed by Barstow at six a.m.

The lack of a message from Mallory didn't necessarily mean anything. She could have forgotten. The reception might be poor.

And he didn't buy it.

The entire team had met soon after arriving and agreed to the protocol. Hourly perimeter sweeps until dusk, then every thirty minutes overnight. Anything suspicious would be reported immediately, to the team, and if possible, to Lifeguard, their point man at headquarters. Check-ins were required, and everyone had a radio. He grabbed his, keyed it, listened for a response.

Beside him, his sweet Aimee moved, then blinked her eyes open. "Everything okay?"

"I'm sure it is."

"But…?"

He didn't believe in hiding things from his clients. As he'd told her earlier, a little fear might keep her sharp. "I didn't get a message from Mallory." He kissed her on the forehead and then climbed from the bed while she gathered the blankets around her.

He dressed hurriedly, grabbed his radio, then tucked his gun into a holster beneath his arm. Before leaving the room, he took a moment to look at her, not sexually, but to communicate how much she mattered to him. "I'll be back in ten minutes." Hopefully less.

"Should I contact my sister?"

"She would want to know. Even if it's nothing." He curled a finger into her hair. "Do not leave the house. My orders are absolute."

She nodded.

"Anything out of the ordinary, contact Lifeguard." All Hawkeye phones were programmed for the assistance. All they had to do was press the number nine and Send.

"Trace…"

At the door, he stopped and looked over his shoulder. "I love you, Aimee. I'll be back for you. Trust no one but me. Promise me."

At his raw, ragged confession, Aimee's heart raced. He… "Trace?"

He was gone.

She hardly heard him descend the staircase or cross the living room, and she doubted she would have known he was gone except for the soft *snick* of the lock on the front door being slid home.

Obeying his last order, she called her sister, then dressed and went downstairs to wait for Trace.

TRACE HAD SPENT TOO MANY YEARS AS A HUNTER NOT TO recognize that faintly metallic smell on the night air. He froze, backed up, got his bearings, adjusted his night vision goggles, then continued on cautiously.

The scent got stronger and stronger as he moved farther away from the cabin.

Then he saw her. Bree Mallory was lying on the ground in a pool of blood. It was a miracle she hadn't already bled out.

Shit.

He fell to his knees.

Her throat had been slit.

"Tried," she whispered. "Tried... Stop him."

He scowled, calculating his options. He needed information and struggled against his instinct to care for her. With the right care she might survive. If he left her alone... *Shit.*

"It was..." She closed her eyes, then managed, "Riley."

He leaned closer to her mouth.

"Go. He can't... Please." Her eyes rolled back, and she gasped, gurgling her own blood.

"Direct pressure, Mallory. That's an order." He grabbed her cell phone and contacted Lifeguard. Because of the GPS location transponder in the phone, he left it with her. "Fucking hang in there."

She faded from consciousness.

Goddamn sonofabitch was going to pay.

SOMETHING SCRATCHED THE WINDOW. AIMEE RATIONALIZED that it could be anything. The wind, an animal, even Trace returning. But when Eureka growled, she knew it was none of those. She moved into the kitchen, keeping her back to the counter. Silently she moved toward the dish drain and grabbed the vicious-looking knife she'd seen Trace use earlier. Then, as silently as she could, she climbed the stairs, then moved to the closet in the farthest bedroom. Her heart was pounding, even though she tried to reassure herself that the sound had been nothing.

Someone pounded on the door. Her first temptation was to answer it, but Trace wouldn't knock, or if he couldn't get in, he'd announce himself. Right?

Huddling behind some clothes, she juggled the knife and the phone. Her hands shook, making the phone waver. It took her three tries to push the number nine and Send. The call took forever to connect, each second dragging into an hour. *Please, please, please answer.*

"Lifeguard. I got you."

She exhaled. Until then, she hadn't realized she'd stopped breathing. "It's Aimee Inamorata. There's someone at the door."

The scratching became louder. Then a window shattered. "Broken…" Fear choked off her words. "Window."

"Help's on the way. We won't let anything happen to you."

The line went dead. She squeezed her eyes shut as she fumbled the useless device. It clattered to the floor. *Fuck.* She froze, paralyzed as the clatter echoed in the silent house.

"I've come for you, Miss Inamorata. Romero sent me. He wants me to bring you to him. He wants you to trust me."

Agent Riley?

For a moment, she almost responded. Instead, she stuffed

156

her hand against her mouth as Trace's words echoed. *"Trust no one."*

"Aimee!"

At Eureka's scream, she clamped her mouth shut. A loud crash ripped through the air, and Eureka shrieked again. "Aimee!"

She fought back tears.

"Trace is hurt!" Riley called. "He needs you."

She gripped the hilt of the knife with both hands.

The unmistakable sound of boots on the wooden stairs made her hands slick. *Be brave. Be brave.*

Her breath strangled her.

"Come out, come out, wherever you are."

Was he certifiable?

"I want you, Miss Inamorata. Only you. You're more valuable than anything. Just come out, and no one else will get hurt. That's what you want. Right?"

No one else will get hurt?

"If you don't want to come out and play, I'll just wait here for Romero. I'll shoot him dead while you watch. It'll be on your head. You want to save him, don't you?"

Trace had asked her to trust him. At the time, she'd had no idea what that would entail. He would come for her. Hawkeye Security would come for her.

"It's you I want." Riley's voice was singsongy. "Come with me. Be a hero. Maybe I'll let your sister live if you give yourself up."

What the hell did he want with her? She had nothing.

Light flooded the room.

She squeezed her eyes shut. She'd had no idea that panic could so completely consume her, shutting down the circuits. She wasn't operating from her higher brain any longer, but from the animalistic part fighting for survival.

Every one of his movements jolted her. The scrape of his shoes on the floor, crashes as he upended or threw things.

Then there was silence, followed by the chill of his laughter as he ripped down what had to be the shower curtain and rod.

"You're running out of places, Aimee, and I'm getting a little mad at you. You don't want me to be mad, do you?"

She swallowed and forced herself to breathe the way she would if she were running. *Dubnium. Dysprosium.* She needed something to stop adrenaline from consuming her. *Einsteinium...* Aimee shook her head. *Einsteinium.*

She could do this.

"Time to come out, Aimee."

Her breaths were shallow, hollow, when he flipped the light switch on in her room. Survival instinct urged her to run. But she was buying seconds.

"Are you under the bed, Aimee?"

At the way he whispered her name, she shuddered, envisioning a million spiders crawling over her.

He was getting closer, his boots on the floor, the sound dragging down her spine. His shadow crept beneath the door, and she fought off her scream.

Riley turned the knob and opened the door a crack. "Come out, come out, wherever you are..."

The barrel of his gun swept inside the closet. Biting her lip, she backed up until the wall stopped any farther retreat.

"I'll bet you're here!" He ripped the door open the rest of the way.

Scared senseless by the sudden motion, she screamed and lashed out, stabbing wildly. She slashed over and over, slashing and gouging, ignoring his shrieks, not caring about anything except getting that gun out of his hand.

"Bitch!" he yelled, reaching in, grabbing her hair, and slamming her head into the wall.

A scream tore across the night.

Not just a scream. A scream from *his woman.*

Consumed with fury, Trace dived through the broken window. Daniel Riley was a dead man.

Gun drawn, Trace moved quickly through the cabin and up the stairs to the back bedroom.

The sight astounded him.

Riley was on his knees, trying to light the oil from a smashed kerosene lamp. Aimee was crawling from the room, drenched in blood. "Trace!"

Fuck. *Yes.* He was damn proud of her.

He leveled his gun at Riley. "Freeze." Trace said

Riley looked up. "I can't lose, Romero. They'll kill me." He dropped the lit match.

His training kicking in, Trace holstered his gun, then grabbed Aimee from the floor and threw her over his shoulder into a fireman's carry before heading down the stairs.

Fighting his fury, Trace headed for the front door, grabbing the birdcage on the way.

Laurents and Barstow emerged from the woods, ripping off their night-vision goggles when they got closer.

"The fuck?" Laurents asked.

"Riley's in there."

"Goddamn. It's your cabin, sir."

"I've got the only two things that matter. He cut up Mallory, left her in the woods. Counterclockwise on the perimeter. Lifeguard has the coordinates." He nodded at Barstow. "Go."

Trace opened the back of his vehicle and set Aimee down, the parrot next to her. Then he grabbed a blanket to wrap her in. Her eyes were wide, and she stared at him, her eyes unfocused. "How bad are you hurt?"

"I don't know." She rubbed her arms. "I just… His blood."

"You did well."

She lapsed into silence and continued to rub her arms. She needed to sort this out, make sense of it any way she could. It would take time and patience, and lots of it.

He smoothed back her hair, and his hand came away covered in her blood.

Within minutes, the sound of sirens pierced the night.

"This time, I'm glad the cavalry is here."

Ms. Inamorata and Torin Carter, a Hawkeye trainer, arrived within minutes. Their speed shouldn't have been possible.

"Carter's in charge of the op from here," she said by way of a greeting. "He'll interface with the authorities and ensure all statements are consistent."

With a tight nod, Torin walked toward Laurents, leaving Trace alone with Ms. Inamorata. She looked as perfect as ever, not a single hair out of place, makeup perfectly blended, and she was in her own version of a uniform, a pencil-slim skirt, feminine blouse, and heels. She carried a briefcase, and there was a smaller bag slung over her shoulder. Rue the man who didn't think she kicked ass and took names.

In the dim light, he saw the betrayal of emotion in her eyes, so like her sister's. Unshakable Inamorata, Hawkeye's right-hand woman, was walking through her worst nightmare. She had to know Aimee would have never been dragged into this if it hadn't been for her. Despite that horror, she'd been making things happen, arranging the cleanup, making sure everyone was taken care of.

"Concussion, most likely, according to the doctor you pulled out of bed," he said without being asked. "Nothing more."

She nodded. "Thank you." She looked over her shoulder at the still-smoldering structure, or what remained of it. "You'll get a new cabin."

"My parents will appreciate it." It gave him satisfaction to know Riley would continue to burn in hell.

"Where is my sister?"

"Back of the Suburban. She's ah…talking to a shrink." He curled his hand in a fist, impatient to be with her.

"I'll get you back by her side in less than ten minutes."

"Five. *Five,* or I'm taking her myself."

"Agent Romero, these things take—"

"Five minutes, Inamorata."

"How bad's the headache?"

Aimee grabbed hold of her sister's voice like the lifeline it had always been. She looked up and gave as much of a smile as she was capable of.

"Family," Inamorata told the counselor, one of their own. "You can have her back tomorrow. Tonight she's ours."

The counselor nodded and left.

"You'll need to be debriefed, all sorts of formalities. I'm sorry."

"I kind of figured."

"Torin Carter's with me. We'll hold off the authorities until tomorrow."

Because of the grief he'd nearly drowned in following his partner's death, Torin was as tough as he was thorough. He'd understand what she was experiencing, as well as what her sister was enduring. Everything he did would protect them both.

"You'll have as many people to talk to for as long as you want. There's going to be no pressure to return to Hawkeye, I promise you that." She gave a ghost of a smile that revealed her pain. "And if you never want to come back, I'm sure there are dozens of Silicon Valley firms that would want you. Hawkeye will give you the best recommendation in history."

"I just don't understand what happened."

"It will take a while to figure it all out. Our guess is that he was a double agent. Russian. Once the injector worked, they wanted the technology. It turns out that Riley volunteered to be on your detail." She exhaled a ragged, short breath. "Also guessing that he broke into your house to cause alarm so that a detail would be assigned."

Aimee wrapped herself even tighter.

"It seems fair to guess that he planned to hold you for ransom. In exchange for the entire software package." She paused. "You stopped him, Aimee."

Despite the blanket, Aimee had never been colder. "Do you know anything about Bree?"

"She's alive." As usual, her sister offered no false promises. "We had her helicoptered out. She's receiving the very best of care."

Aimee didn't ask anything else.

"I'm afraid Trace has only given me five minutes with you…something about coming after you himself otherwise."

"He would too."

"This is about you, Little Sis. If you don't want him, he'll be gone."

"I think I like him."

The sisters exchanged smiles. Then tears swam in Inamorata's eyes. "Jesus, Aimee… I'm sorry."

"You couldn't have known." This was the first time in

their lives that she'd been the one to soothe her big sister. They held hands, and Aimee repeated, "You couldn't have known."

"I'm supposed to keep you safe."

Aimee accepted the comfort when her sibling wrapped an arm around her shoulder. They were still like that when Trace rejoined them.

"Scram," he told Inamorata.

"Silver-tongued devil," she said.

"I want the nicest hotel room in Winter Park."

"It's yours. You'll have a text message with directions."

Aimee was stunned, and not just from the blow to the head. Her sister was taking orders from Trace, and she seemed happy to be doing it.

The dynamic astounded her. Her sister had always looked out for her, now she was not so voluntarily abdicating the position.

"Here's a bag of stuff you might need, extra clothes, toiletries. They're my clothes, so they're probably too big, but Trace will take you shopping tomorrow."

"And Hawkeye will pay the bill," he added.

"Of course." She started to walk away. Then she stopped and looked back. "Take care of her."

By the time she'd finished the sentence, he'd scooped Aimee into his arms. With a soft sigh, she laid her head on his shoulder. "I could stay here all night."

"I have other ideas for you."

"Do you?"

"The doctor suggested I wake you up a number of times through the night to check on you. Any ideas how I should do that?"

"Maybe one or two, Agent Romero. Maybe one or two."

EPILOGUE

HAWKEYE

"Tie me up?"

"Aimee…" His woman, his lover, had him exactly where she wanted him. When she was naked on her knees in front of him, he could deny her nothing. When she did *that* with her tongue to the tip of his bare cock…

She'd been wanting to scene, and so far he'd been heroic enough to resist her. The scar on the side of her head still bothered him, and she'd told him, more than once, to get over himself.

Every day, he relived the nightmare of nearly losing her. "It's too soon."

"It's not." She gave his balls a squeeze that made him catch his breath. "I want you to bend me over the bed, Sir."

The image alone was enough to nearly make him come.

"I want you to fuck me hard."

The rest of her sentence went unfinished. *Like you used to.*

She gave his shaft a long, loving lick. "Trust *me*, Trace. I'm okay."

"Aimee, I'm warning you."

She looked up at him earnestly. "This isn't working for me."

His heart stopped. Those were the words he lived in dread of hearing. They'd spent the last three weeks on the Southern California coast in a beach house provided by their employer. Trace had wanted to take her out of the country, but she wouldn't leave Eureka behind.

Except for having the bird with them, the first two weeks had been perfect, with long walks on the beach, hitting all the tourist traps, feeding her at all the restaurants. But the last one had been more volatile. As her strength returned and the nightmares stopped, she wanted their sex life to return to what she called normal.

For the last week, they'd argued every day. She accused him of treating her like porcelain. She was right. And so what of it? He was going to keep her safe and protected, even from him.

"I've tried it your way." She sat back on her heels, dropping her hands to her thighs. "I want it to be like it was."

"I nearly fucking lost you." He reached for her, willing her to understand his pain.

"Do it! Do it," she shouted. "Grab my hair."

He sighed and dropped his hand.

"Except for that, everything's perfect."

"So leave it alone, damn it."

"No! Because without that, it's not real. We're not real." She sat back on her heels. "You kept asking me to trust you when it came to BDSM, to Riley. Now you need to trust yourself. Trust me. Trust me to set the limits, trust me to let you know if I can't do it, trust me to let you know if it's too much."

"You were at the hands of a madman."

"And I kicked his ass."

He laughed.

166

"Well, that's my story, and I'm sticking to it. And I'll kick yours too, if you treat me badly. Don't you get it? That freak wins if he steals what we had."

"You've been seeing a shrink."

"It's not psychobabble. It's the truth. We stopped him from stealing the technology. We have to stop him from stealing this from us."

"I'm afraid of hurting you."

"If you do, I'll tell you."

"We'll do this my way."

She sighed. "This feels familiar."

"When we return to Denver, it will be with my ring on your finger." He dug his hands into her hair.

"Wait—"

"My way, Aimee."

"My sister's right. You are a silver-tongued devil. Was that a proposal?"

"No. It was a statement of fact."

"I'm marrying you?"

He steeled himself as he fought to tamp down his doubts, fears. This wasn't the way he'd planned to propose. He wanted a ring and flowers, romance, a wonderful dinner, a carriage ride. Instead, he'd panicked, afraid she would refuse him. "Within six months."

"That night…"

"I said I loved you." And he'd had no idea how much until he almost lost her. He took her shoulders and drew her up. "You're the only one. The only woman I've ever loved."

"Oh, Trace." She stroked his cheek. He'd made her life complete. "I can't imagine a future without you."

"Tell me you love me." He dug his fingers into her hair gently.

"There's never been anyone else for me." She surrendered

instantly, turning her head into the cradle of his palm. "I love you, Trace."

"I'm never letting you go. I'm applying for a job at headquarters. I should be home more than I'm gone."

"I want us to live at my house."

"Or something bigger, eventually. For now that's fine."

"And I want to keep Bella."

"I thought we discussed that. I'm the Dom."

"Bella! Bella!"

He glanced over at the two annoying-as-hell parrots. They'd been at the beach a couple of days ago, and there'd been an animal-adoption booth set up as part of a city festival. She'd fallen in love with a parrot that needed a home. The rescue people weren't sure how Bella would do with another parrot, but Aimee had begged all of them to let her give it a try, and what Aimee wanted, she got. He was putty in her hands, and he was afraid she knew it.

They were closing in on the end of the trial period. Now it seemed he'd end up with two of the flying idiots. It confounded him how two parrots could make five times the noise of one.

"Uhm, theoretically Eureka won't be as possessive of me if he has a mate."

"Everything with that loco is theoretical. Idiot that he is, he'll probably think he's in a ménage."

"Isn't the Spanish word for parrot *loro*, not *loco?*"

"Whatever."

"Tie me up. Fuck me."

He tightened his grip in her hair, and she closed her eyes on a soft sigh.

"Take me…" She looked up at him and licked her lower lips seductively. "Take me, *Sir.*"

"Over that chair, sub. Legs spread, your cunt exposed, your hands gripping the chair legs."

He'd thrown her off balance, he saw. She'd pictured what she wanted, but how badly did she really want what they'd had?

"Yes, Trace," she whispered.

"You may crawl."

She blinked. "Yes, Trace."

His cock hardened even more. She draped herself over the chair as he'd instructed. And now, for both of them, there was one last test. "Point your toes in." She was experienced enough to realize that would just make her presentation that much more erotic. He left her there for long minutes, enjoying the view. She shifted position slightly a couple of times, but she didn't protest or try to stand. He gave her every opportunity to call a halt to this, and all she did was sway her hips seductively.

He moved around her deliberately, using soft cuffs to secure her in place.

He dipped a hand between her legs and found her wet for him, wetter than she'd ever been for him.

In the distance, he was aware of the surf. In here, he was aware of the roar of the blood in his ears.

He sheathed his cock with a condom and took her. Hard. Fast. Digging one hand into her hair, supporting her with another, he pounded, pistoning, penetrating deeper and deeper.

"Yes! I want you. Fuck me. Fuck me *harder*. Now."

She was a demanding little sub, and she was all his.

Without permission, screaming, Aimee came.

Within seconds, way ahead of his planned schedule, he groaned loudly as he ejaculated. Satisfied, he slapped her rear as he pulled out. "You made me come too quickly." He spanked her flank again, and she stunned him by whispering, "Thank you."

He released the cuffs and carried her to the bed.

She curled up next to him, in the protection of his arms. Together, they looked out at the ocean, to the future.

Aimee turned back to him. He focused on the tiny scar on her forehead, but this time, he saw it was healing, maybe like they were. They had a future ahead of them. He was determined they would savor every beautiful moment of it.

"Kiss me?" she whispered.

"Querida, that's only the beginning of what I'm going to do to you."

She offered her mouth, and he accepted her sweet, forever invitation.

Thank you for reading Trust in Me. I hope you had fun with Trace and Aimee. (And of course Eureka!) Hawkeye and his agents have a very special place in my heart. For the men of Hawkeye, the line of duty between bodyguard and client isn't meant to be crossed.

Spend time with your next irresistible Hawkeye agent in Meant For Me. As his trainee, Mira was far too young and much too innocent for Torin's carnal demands. And now she's been assigned as his partner, placing her firmly in the forbidden category.

Even though she hated him for pushing her so hard during training, Mira has always been attracted to the older, sexy-as-sin Hawkeye commander.

Despite the danger swirling around them, Mira is a temptation Torin can't resist.

DISCOVER MEANT FOR ME

If you love sexy, dangerous cowboys, be sure to read Hold On To Me now. He was supposed to protect her, not fall in love.

Hawkeye needs help protecting a woman he cares about. Former operative Jacob Walker can't refuse one last mission, even if the beautiful, fiery woman wants nothing to do with him.

But the overwhelming alpha is resolute. Elissa finds herself thrown over the shoulder of the inflexible bodyguard and kidnapped, taken to his remote ranch, where she discovers something even more dangerous—her attraction to her smoking-hot captor.

★★★★★ Super hot and super sexy! Love these two!!!
~Amazon Reviewer

DISCOVER HOLD ON TO ME

Turn the page for an exciting excerpt from Meant For Me

MEANT FOR ME
CHAPTER ONE EXCERPT

PROLOGUE

"What do you think?"

From his place on the raised platform that had once served as a fire outlook post, Torin Carter glanced at Hawkeye, his boss and mentor. The man owned the security firm Torin worked for, as well as this eight-hundred-acre outpost in the remote part of the West. "Think of what? The class?"

Six times a year, recruits new to the VIP protection program cycled through the Aiken Training Facility. It wasn't Torin's job to get them through. It was his job to make sure that everyone, except the very best, washed out.

"That recruit in specific. Going through the bog." Aviator glasses shaded Hawkeye's eyes as well as his thoughts.

"Mira Araceli?" Torin asked.

"That's the one."

Carrying a thirty-pound pack, face smeared with mud, her training uniform soaked, Mira Araceli dashed at full-out speed toward the next obstacle. She grabbed the rope and began to pull herself up the ten-foot wall as if she hadn't just navigated a killer course designed to destroy her energy reserves.

Today, her long-black hair with its deep fiery highlights was not only in a ponytail, it was tucked inside her jacket. She concentrated on the task in front of her, never looking away from her goal.

Torin had been running the training program for several years. During that time, only a few recruits stood out. "She's…" He searched for words to convey his conflict. Brave. Relentless. Driven, by something she'd never talked about during the admission process.

On a couple of occasions, he'd studied her file. Hawkeye's comprehensive background check had turned up nothing out of the ordinary. Youngest of three kids. Her father was a congressman and former military. Both of her brothers had followed his legacy—and expectations?—into the service.

Araceli's academic scores were excellent. She'd graduated in the top of her college class but had opted not to put her skills to use in a safe corporate environment. Instead, she'd applied to be part of Hawkeye Security, even though she knew the scope of their work, from protecting people and things, to operating in some of the most difficult places on the planet. *Why does she want to put her life at risk?*

Fuck. Why did anyone?

Hawkeye cleared his throat.

Torin glanced back at his boss. "She's one of the most determined I've ever seen. Works harder than anyone. Longer hours." Yesterday he'd hit the gym at five a.m. She was already there, wearing a sports bra beneath a sheer gray tank top. Rather than workout pants, she opted for formfitting shorts that showed off her toned legs and well-formed rear. They exchanged polite greetings, and she'd wandered over to be his spotter for his bench presses, then offered a hand up when he was done.

He shouldn't have accepted. But he had. A sensation, dormant for years, had sparked. Raw sexual attraction for Mira Araceli had shot straight to his cock, a violation of his personal ethics.

She hadn't pulled away like she should have. Her palms were callused, and so much smaller than his. Torin was smart enough to recognize her danger, though. He'd honed her strength himself. She would have him flat on his back anytime she wanted.

In the distance, a door slammed, and they moved away from each other. From across the room, he saw her looking at her hand.

No doubt she'd experienced the same electric pulse as he did.

Since that morning, he'd been damn sure she wasn't in the gym before he entered. Relationships among Hawkeye operatives weren't expressly forbidden. Hawkeye was smart enough to know that close quarters, adrenaline, fear, and survival instincts were a powerful cocktail. But the relationship between a recruit and instructors was sacred.

Having sex with Araceli wouldn't just be stupid—it would border on insane.

In addition to the fact that he was responsible for her safety, Araceli was far too young for his carnal demands. And it wasn't just in terms of age. Life had dealt him a vicious blow, leaving parts of him in jagged pieces.

He no longer even pretended to be relationship material.

When he could, he went to a BDSM club. There, he found women who wanted the same things he did. Extreme. Extreme enough to round the edges off the memories, the past.

There was no way he would subject a recruit to the

danger that he represented, even if she was tempting as hell.

Hawkeye was still waiting, and Torin settled for a nonanswer. "Her potential is unlimited."

"But?" Hawkeye folded his arms. Despite the thirty-seven-degree temperature, he'd skipped a coat and opted for a sweatshirt to go with his customary black khakis. Combined with his aviator glasses and black ball cap embroidered with the Hawkeye logo, the company owner was incognito.

Torin looked at her again. "She does best in situations where she is by herself." And that wasn't how Hawkeye Security operated. They believed no person was better alone than as part of a team. Certainly there were times when an agent had no backup and was left with no choice but to take individual action. But the ability to work with others was crucial to success.

"What do you think of her chances?"

Torin shrugged. When she first joined Hawkeye a year ago, she'd trained at the Tactical Operations Center. She could pump thirty-seven out of forty shots into a target's heart and was first through the door during hostage rescue exercises. Though she'd excelled, she took unnecessary risks. At times, she calculatingly ignored superiors' commands. So far it had worked well for her, much to the annoyance of her numerous instructors.

On her application to the program that Torin headed, she'd indicated she had too much downtime during her assignments. She wanted something more demanding. VIP protection could provide that. If she made it.

Araceli summited a second wall, then leaped off and kept moving, dropping down to crawl through a tunnel, then back up to navigate the ridiculously tough agility course.

Hawkeye watched her progress. "There's something about her."

At the end of the course, she doubled over to catch her breath; then she checked her time on a fitness watch. Only then did she shrug off the pack.

"Lots of potential," Torin agreed.

"Either hone it or get her out of here." Hawkeye adjusted his ball cap. "They'd be glad to have her back in tactical. And with her IQ scores, she'd do well in a support role. Strategy."

She was a little young for that.

Then again, age wasn't always a factor. He knew that more than most.

"You doing okay?" Hawkeye asked.

Torin twitched. "It's easier."

In his usual way, Hawkeye remained silent, letting time and tension stretch, waiting.

"I think about it every day." Dreams. Nightmares. Second-guessing himself, his reactions, replaying it and never changing the outcome.

"You've accumulated plenty of time off."

"I'd rather work."

"Understood."

Torin and Hawkeye watched a couple more recruits finish the course. Results were fed through to his high-tech tablet. Not surprisingly, Mira had finished in the top three.

In the distance, an old bus lumbered toward them, spewing a cloud of dirt in its wake.

Turning his head to watch it, Hawkeye asked, "You heading to Aiken Junction?"

"Yeah." Torin grinned. Drills in the mock town were one of his favorite parts of being an instructor. And he fully intended to use the opportunity to be sure Araceli learned a valuable lesson. "Want to join us?"

"If I had time." Hawkeye sighed. "Another damn dinner. Another damn meeting with a multinational company." Hawkeye wasn't just the founder and owner of the security firm—he was their best performing salesperson. "And I'm going to get the account."

"Never doubted you, boss."

Hawkeye clapped Torin on the shoulder. "I've taken enough of your day."

After nodding, Torin descended the steps, then jogged over to the finish line where recruits were talking, drinking water, dreaming about a beer or the hot tub. "Listen up!"

Talking ceased.

"You're responsible for protecting the family of an important diplomat. Their youngest daughter is seventeen and just slipped her security detail. And you're going to get her back."

There were groans and resigned sighs. The group had hit the running track at six a.m., had hours of classroom instruction, missed lunch, and been timed on their run through the mud challenge. And their day was just beginning.

He pointed to the approaching vehicle. "Gear up."

Exhausted recruits picked up the packs they'd just shucked.

"The bus will stop for ninety seconds. If you're not on it, you'll be hiking to Aiken Junction."

Mira grabbed a protein bar from her bag then slung it over one shoulder. She made sure she was first on the bus and moved to a seat farthest in the back.

Torin jumped on as the driver dropped the transmission into gear. While others had doubled up and were chatting, Araceli leaned forward and draped a T-shirt over her head. Smart. She was taking time to recover mentally and physically.

"Here's the drill." He stood at the top of the stairwell, holding on to a pole as the ancient vehicle hit every damn rock and pothole, jarring his jaw. "The tattoo parlor denied her because she's underage, and the artist we interviewed said he saw her move over to Thump, the nightclub next to

Bones." The name of their fictitious high-end steakhouse. "She has a fake ID, so it's possible she got past security. Her daddy wants her home, and wants her safe. This isn't the first time she's slipped her detail. You'll stage at the church. Choose a team leader and make a plan. Any questions?"

Most people lapsed into silence, a few engaged in banter and trash talk, and he took a seat behind the driver.

A mind-numbing thirty minutes later, the bus churned through Hell's Acre, the seedy area of town, then crossed the fake railroad tracks that separated the sleazy area of town from the more respectable suburban setting.

The driver braked to a grinding halt in front of the clapboard All Saints Church.

"Not so fast," Torin said when the recruits began to stand. "This isn't your stop."

He jogged down the steps to the sidewalk, and the driver pulled the lever to shut the door, then hit the accelerator fast enough to cause the occupants some whiplash—good training for real-life evasive driving. The recruits would be taken around the town several times in order to give Torin and the role-players time to set up.

Once the bus disappeared from view, he pulled open the door to the restaurant and entered the dining room where he greeted fellow instructors. "Who's playing our principal?"

"That's me, Commander." Charlotte Bixby—four feet eleven, ninety-two pounds, and ferocious as a man twice her size—waved from the back of the room. She wore a black dress and flats that would give her some maneuverability.

"And your gentlemen friends?"

Two agents raised their hands.

Torin went through the rest of the roles, couples, bartenders, cocktail servers, DJ Asylum, partiers on the dance floor. All in all, over two dozen people were assigned to the scene. "Okay, people! Let's head over."

Twenty minutes later, music blared. Charlotte was seated in a booth attached to the far wall. She was wedged between two solid men, a cocktail in front of her. The dance floor in the center of the room was filled with gyrating couples, servers moved around the room, and a bartender was drawing a beer. The surveillance room was being manned by one of the instructors, and he was wearing a polo shirt that identified him as one of Thump's security team. The bouncer, nicknamed Bear, was dressed similarly, but wearing a jacket that emphasized his broad shoulders and beefy biceps. Arms folded, Torin stood behind Bear.

Since a cold front was moving through and the temperature had dropped to just above freezing, a coat check had been set up near the front door, close to the restrooms.

Everything was in place.

A role player sashayed through the front door and gave Bear a once-over and an inviting smile. That didn't stop him from scrutinizing her ID.

"Enjoy your evening, Miss."

After snatching her ID back, she breezed past them and headed straight for the bar.

Several more people entered, and none of them were Hawkeye recruits. Hopefully that meant they were still strategizing. He preferred that to seeing them head in without a plan…like they had last time they ran a similar drill.

He checked his watch.

Fifteen minutes.

Then thirty.

Charlotte was on her second cocktail.

An hour.

Torin left the door to grab a beer at the bar. Then he carried it to the side of the room and stood at a tall round table.

DJ Asylum turned on pulsing colored strobe lights and cranked up the music. The walls echoed from the bass. People shouted to be heard.

Exactly like an ordinary bar in Anytown, USA.

One of Charlotte's companions signaled for another drink and then draped that arm across her back. She leaned into him.

Within minutes, Araceli strolled in. Her face was clean, and she'd changed into clean clothes—obviously they'd been in her backpack, along with a shiny headband. Nothing could hide her combat boots, though.

Life wasn't a series of perfect opportunities. Blending in mattered, but speed was critical. It did mean that the role players had an advantage, though.

Along with a fellow trainee, Araceli found a table. Instead of waiting for a cocktail waitress, she headed to the bar. She scanned the occupants, saw him, gave no acknowledgment that they'd ever met.

Yeah. Hawkeye was right. She was damn good.

She secured two drinks, then, instead of heading back to the table, walked to the far end of the room and began a search for their principal.

Smart. She wouldn't approach right away, she'd make sweep, assess the situation, all the while looking as if she fit in.

Except for those ridiculous combat boots.

Under the flashing lights, he lost her. Until her headband winked in the light.

He checked out the other recruits and their strategies. Two of them—women—looped arms like besties and pretended to look for men.

DJ Asylum's voice boomed through the room, distorted by some sort of synthesizer. "Get on the floor and show me your moves!"

One of the trainers walked to the table where Charlotte sat and whispered into the ear of the man with his arm draped over her shoulder.

Araceli put down her drink.

The companion nodded and moved his arm to reach into his pocket. Money exchanged hands.

The second guy slid off his seat, effectively blocking the pathway to the booth.

The man Charlotte was cozying up to led her to the dance floor. Araceli stood, looked around for a male agent, grabbed him, then pulled him toward the other couple.

Moments later, fog spilled from machines, clouding the air.

Lights went out, and the music stopped so abruptly that it seemed to thunder off the still-pulsating walls.

It took a few seconds for emergency lighting to kick on. When it did, the fog was thick and surreal, and Charlotte and her dance partner were gone.

Araceli headed toward the exit and shoved her way past Bear and out of the building.

Torin strolled toward the coatroom. He pushed the door most of the way closed, leaving a crack so he could watch the front door.

Moments later, Araceli hurried back in, her winking headband all but a neon sign indicating her position. He eased the door open, then, as she started past, reached out, grabbed her, pulled her in, and caught her in a rear hold, an elbow under her chin, his right arm beneath her breasts.

She was breathing hard, but she grabbed his forearms to try to break free. In response, he tightened the hold to ward off an elbow jab. And he leaned her forward to prevent one of her vicious, calculated stomps. "Knock it off, Araceli," he growled into her ear.

"Commander Carter?" She froze. "It's dark. How did you know it was me?"

"Your headband."

"Shit."

"That's right. You lose." He loosened his grip slightly, but she kept her hands in place. "Your target is gone."

With a deep, frustrated sigh, she tipped her head back, resting it on his chest. And he noticed her. The way she fit with him, and how she trusted him, despite her annoyance at having been bested. And even the way she smelled...wildflowers and innocence, despite the grueling ordeal earlier today. He wanted to reassure her, let her know how proud he was of her efforts.

Jesus. Immediately he released her. He'd held her longer than he need to. Longer than he should have. "Go to Bones. I'll meet you there." Torin took a step back, literal as well as mental.

In the near dark, she faced him. "But I can—"

"Go. I'm one of the bad guys, Araceli." And not just for the role-playing scenario. He was no good for her. "I took you out of the game. You never even noticed me. You didn't make a plan. You rushed forward without assessing the situation. You failed."

After a few seconds of hesitation, she nodded. "It will be the last time, Commander Carter. You underestimate me and my capabilities."

Something he didn't want to name snaked through him.

She had to be talking about the job, nothing more. Araceli couldn't know about his inner turmoil and his dark attraction to her.

Alone in the dark, Torin balled his hand into a fist over and over, opening, closing. Opening. Closing.

By far, Mira Araceli was the most dangerous student he'd ever had.

CHAPTER ONE

"You all right, Mira?"

For three years, six months, and twelve days, Torin Carter had haunted Mira Araceli's days and teased her nights.

Jonathan, the personal trainer she worked with when she was staying in New Orleans, snapped his fingers in front of her face. "Mira?"

His proximity, along with the sharp sound, finally broke through her runaway thoughts, and she shook head to clear it of the distraction that was her former Hawkeye instructor.

What the hell was wrong with her? She shouldn't have checked out mentally, even for a fraction of a second. In the wrong circumstances, it could mean the difference between survival and death. "Sorry." With a smile meant to be reassuring, she met his eyes.

For most of her life, she'd practiced yoga. Five years ago, she'd learned to meditate. Yet when it came to Torin, she never remembered to use her skills.

"Something on your mind?"

"Was. There was. I'm good to go now." She was almost done with the final set—squatting over two hundred pounds. She could do this. *Right?* In a couple of minutes, she'd be out of here and headed for the house where she would spend the next nine weeks living with her nemesis.

How the hell had this even happened? Hawkeye required all instructors—even the head of the program—to spend time in the field to keep their skills sharp. But for them to be assigned to the same team…?

"Ready?" Jonathan asked. "You have three more reps."

With single-minded focus, she tucked way thoughts of her demanding and mysterious former instructor.

Jonathan scowled. "You sure everything's okay?"

She got in position, adjusted her grip, then took a breath.

"Hold up." He nudged one of her feet.

"Thanks." After executing the squat, watching her form, breathing correctly, she racked the bar and stepped away. No matter what she wanted to believe, thoughts of Torin had wormed past her defenses to dominate her thoughts. "I'm calling it."

Jonathan nodded. "Good plan." He checked his clipboard. "See you back the day after tomorrow?"

"Six a.m. I won't miss it." She grabbed her water bottle, took a swig, then headed for the locker room. This was the first time in her adult life that she'd cut a workout short.

Mira showered, then took longer than normal with her makeup. Long enough to piss her off. Frustrated, she shoved the cap back onto her lipstick and dropped it in her bag.

Even though she routinely had male partners, she wasn't in the habit of primping. Of course, she'd never had an all-consuming attraction to one of them before.

Torin Carter wasn't just gorgeous. As her VIP Protective Services instructor, he'd been tougher on her than anyone ever had been, demanding her very best, harshly grading her work. It was his job to make her a stellar agent or cut her from the program. He hadn't known that failure was never a possibility.

During her training, he'd never shown anything beyond a hard-ass, impersonal interaction toward her. Except for that night at Thump.

When he'd caught her in that choke hold, she'd struggled, elbowing him, attempting to stomp on his foot. His commanding voice had subdued her, and when she stopped struggling, she noticed his arms around her.

Even though he loosened his hold, Torin didn't release her right away like other instructors had. And in a reaction that was wholly unlike her, she tipped her head back and relaxed into him, seeking comfort, a brief respite from the relentless and grueling training exercises. For a moment, she forgot about her job, stopped noticing the fog and pandemonium around them.

She thought—maybe—that he experienced an echoing flare, but he pushed her away, with a harsh indictment of her skills.

Drowning in rejection and embarrassment, she squared her shoulders and locked away her ridiculous unrequited emotions and vowed never to examine them again.

Even though she'd graduated years ago and hadn't heard his name since, he was never far away. Frustratingly, she thought of him every time she went out on a date. It was as if her subconscious was weighing and measuring all men against him.

The comparisons even happened when she scened at a BDSM club.

Torin was everything she wanted a Dom to be—uncompromising, strong, intelligent...and, at the right time, reassuring. In his arms, in that coatroom, she'd discovered he was capable of tenderness. Maybe if she'd only seen him be an ass, he would have been easier to forget.

Surviving Torin might be her greatest test ever.

Mira dragged her hair back over her shoulder and stared at herself in the mirror. "You." She pointed at her reflection. "You're smarter this time. Wiser. More in control."

A blonde emerged from one of the shower stalls. "Man problems?"

Embarrassed, Mira lifted a shoulder. She hadn't realized her words would be overheard.

"Isn't it always?" the woman asked.

For other people, not her. "That's the thing. It never has been until now."

"I see you here all the time. You're tough. Whatever it is, you can handle it."

Mira hoped so. She smiled at the other woman. "Thank you. I needed that pep talk." After blotting her lipstick, she gathered her belongings, exited the gym, then strode across the parking lot to her car.

She and Torin were scheduled to rendezvous at seven p.m. at Hawkeye's mansion in the Garden District. Since it was equipped with modern security both inside and out, he preferred his high-value clients utilize it when they visited NOLA. In addition to eight bedrooms, there was a spacious carriage house apartment for use by security personnel.

The grounds were spectacular, with a large outdoor swimming pool, a concrete courtyard with plenty of lounge chairs, tables, and umbrellas. Potted plants provided splashes of color, while numerous trees offered privacy as well as shade.

She'd stayed on the property several times, including earlier this year for Mardi Gras while she was working the detail for an A-list actor. She planned to arrive before Torin so she could select her bedroom, get settled, have the upper hand. Any advantage, no matter how small, was a necessity.

Since it was still early afternoon, she managed the traffic with only the usual snarls.

After passing the biometric security system at the gate, she drove onto the property.

More confident now, she grabbed her gear, then jogged up the stairs to enter the code on the keypad. A moment later, the lock turned, and she opened the door.

Torin stood in the middle of the main living space, arms folded, damn biceps bulging. His rakishly long black hair was damp, and the atmosphere sizzled with his scent, that of crisp moonlit nights. He swept his gaze over her, and it took all her concentration to remain in place as he assessed her with his shockingly bluc eyes.

When he tipped his head to the side, reaction flooded her.

Her knees wobbled, and she dropped her duffel bag off her shoulder and lowered her gear to the hardwood floor to disguise her too-real, too-feminine reaction.

"I won't bite." His grin was quick and lethal.

Damn him. Part of her wished he would. It might help get rid of the tension crawling through her so she could move on, forget him. There was no way any man could be as hot as she believed he would be. Was there?

*Read more of **Meant For Me.***

ABOUT THE AUTHOR

I invite you to be the very first to know all the news by subscribing to my very special VIP Reader newsletter! You'll find exclusive excerpts, bonus reads, and insider information. https://www.sierracartwright.com/subscribe/

For tons of fun and to meet other awesome people like you, join my Facebook reader group: https://www.facebook.com/groups/SierrasSuperStars And for a current booklist, please visit my website www.sierracartwright.com

International bestselling author Sierra Cartwright was born in England, and she spent her early childhood traipsing through castles and dreaming of happily-ever afters. She was raised in Colorado and now calls Galveston, Texas home. She loves to connect with her readers, so please feel free to drop her a note.

facebook.com/SierraCartwrightOfficial
instagram.com/sierracartwrightauthor
bookbub.com/authors/sierra-cartwright

Donovan Dynasty

Bind

Brand

Boss

Mastered

With This Collar

On His Terms

Over The Line

In His Cuffs

For The Sub

In The Den

Made in United States
North Haven, CT
19 November 2021

11287137R00108